# DEATH BY SUDOKU

# DEATH BY SUDOKU

## KAYE MORGAN

**WHEELER**
**CHIVERS**

This Large Print edition is published by Wheeler Publishing, Waterville, Maine, USA and by BBC Audiobooks Ltd, Bath, England.

Wheeler Publishing is an imprint of The Gale Group.

Wheeler is a trademark and used herein under license.

The text of this Large Print edition is unabridged.

Other aspects of the book may vary from the original edition.

Set in 16 pt. Plantin.

---

**LIBRARY OF CONGRESS CATALOGING-IN-PUBLICATION DATA**

Morgan, Kaye.
    Death by sudoku / by Kaye Morgan.
        p. cm. — (A sudoku mystery) (Wheeler Publishing large print cozy mystery)
    ISBN-13: 978-1-59722-654-7 (alk. paper)
    ISBN-10: 1-59722-654-8 (alk. paper)
    1. Sudoku — Fiction. 2. Puzzles — Fiction. 3. Murder — Fiction.
4. Oregon — Fiction. 5. Large type books. I. Title.
PS3613.O7454D43 2007
813'.6—dc22                                                    2007033562

---

BRITISH LIBRARY CATALOGUING-IN-PUBLICATION DATA AVAILABLE

Published in 2007 in the U.S. by arrangement with The Berkley Publishing Group, a member of Penguin Group (USA) Inc.
Published in 2008 in the U.K. by arrangement with Penguin Group (USA) Inc.

U.K. Hardcover: 978 1 405 64334 4 (Chivers Large Print)
U.K. Softcover: 978 1 405 64335 1 (Camden Large Print)

Printed in the United States of America on permanent paper
10 9 8 7 6 5 4 3 2 1

This book is dedicated with love to Mom, my first reader, who always tells the truth. I love her anyway.

And no acknowledgments would be complete without thanks to the person who made it possible. To my editor at Berkley, Samantha Mandor, who not only championed this book, but also had a very large hand in creating this world and its characters.

■ ■ ■ ■

# PART ONE:
# NAKED PAIRS

■ ■ ■ ■

Don't get excited by the name. In sudoku, naked pairs are hardly X-rated — in fact, they don't even rate a hard R. The name refers to a situation in a row, column, or box where two spaces have the same two choices (and only the same two choices) as candidates. The naked part is because they're right out there in the open. It's an either-or situation. Logically, if the choice is between a 2 or a 4, a 2 in the first space means a 4 in the second. It also means that 2s and 4s can be eliminated from the candidate lists everywhere else in the

given row, column, or box. Those numbers
have been taken already . . .
      — Excerpt from *Sudo-cues* by Liza K

# 1

*Just keep your head down and sit tight,* Liza Kelly told herself for the umpteenth time as she hunched in her seat. *The screaming will have to stop soon.* The two-and-a-half-hour flight had reached the halfway mark. These kids had to be getting tired by now.

Liza was taking the trip from Oregon to Southern California for business — well, she was hoping this sudoku tournament would advance her career. Unfortunately, most (like 99 percent) of the other passengers for sunny Orange County had another destination in mind — Disneyland. And 100 percent of these vacationers had small children in tow.

The 737 had been reasonably quiet at first. Yes, the kids had been excited, but they were also sleepy. Arriving three hours before a 7:15 a.m. flight would do that to most people. For Liza, driving to Portland from beautiful downtown Maiden's Bay, that had meant leaving an additional hour in advance, getting up and traveling in the kind of wee hours she hadn't seen since she was in college pulling all-nighters. At least now she knew why she didn't remember them very well. It was hard to hold things in your memory when your vision was too blurry to see them clearly in the first place.

She'd somehow dragged herself to the car, cleared her driveway, and gotten on the road. But Liza quickly realized that she'd never win the race to get to PDX in time for baggage searches and whatever — not without a serious infusion of coffee.

But in the tiny town where she lived, twenty-four-hour convenience stores were in short supply — nonexistent, in fact. Liza's luck had been in. She'd been able to grab a cup of sludgy coffee (probably yesterday's brew) at Ma's Café in beautiful downtown Maiden's Bay. Ma hadn't been there, but her son Calvin had just been opening the doors when Liza pulled up. It had taken him a couple of attempts to get the key in. That, combined with the awful hour, suggested to Liza that he'd come searching for some sort of hangover cure. At least, whatever was in his cup had smelled more medicinal than tasty. Halfway through this trip, Liza wished he'd made one of whatever that was up for her, too, packed to go.

Her head had been pounding since the plane hit cruising altitude — and the change in cabin pressure hit the ears of each and every toddler aboard at the same time. They didn't know what was going on, but they definitely didn't like it. Their befuddled parents hadn't known how to make things better, and the cabin crew had apparently gone into hiding.

Liza knew. She'd looked for them. After failing to find them, she had just sat and suffered. And observed the situation.

She figured that the little boy beside her might have a great career ahead of him in opera, based on his volume and ability to hold a note. When he'd finally paused in his vocal output, Liza had glanced over in surprise, wondering what had caused the silence. The little guy had raised his head from his dozing (exhausted) mother's shoulder to look around. A tear made a trail down his plump cheek, and another shimmered in his incredibly long eyelashes. His lips quivered as he recovered from his prolonged crying jag.

Liza basically liked kids, even faced with an army of screaming ones. She managed a sympathetic smile for the miniature Pavarotti. Her friendly response diverted him from another outburst. Instead, he made a grab and snagged the floppy hat sitting in her lap. Liza had tossed the hat and a pair of large sunglasses into her carry-on as she left her house. She had felt the need for some Hollywood camouflage heading back down to the Greater L.A. area — you never knew when you were going to bump into somebody from The Business.

She smiled to herself. The Business — as if there were only one in Southern California.

The little guy to her right took the smile as encouragement. Peering at her over the brim of her hat, he raised it up and started a game of peekaboo. Liza's looks of extravagant surprise whenever his eyes came into view delighted her young playmate.

He lowered the hat and grinned at her, showing off four brand-new teeth, and leaned over to pat her hand. The difference in their skin tones fascinated the little guy — his tiny fingers pale and pink against the muted ivory of her untanned palm. Liza smiled at the sudden memory of a college boyfriend's extravagant description of her as a "golden Oriental princess." There was maybe 50 percent truth in that. Certainly, she was only 50 percent Oriental — or

Asian as the PC crowd was just beginning to say in those days. The rest of her was pure Irish, from the reddish streaks in her hair to her temper.

Her little friend rooted around in the seat beside him to come up with a treasure. He held out the baby book, turning the heavy cardboard pages to an inset plastic mirror. After peering myopically into it, he handed it to her. Liza played the game, looking at a sort of fun-house mirror image of herself, thanks to the slightly warped plastic. Her high cheekbones, a Kelly legacy, ballooned before her, along with the proud nose bequeathed by some Norman ancestor. The rest of her face was pure Watanabe — almond-shaped brown eyes and a mouth that was a little wider than traditional standards of beauty. "Big," her obnoxious older brother had often told her. As for the rest of the package, well, she'd always considered her figure sturdy, but another college boyfriend had amended that to "curvy."

Little Pavarotti graciously accepted the book back. Then he reached out again, this time going for her hair. Liza glanced at dozing Mom. The baby's mom had a short, blond bob. The little guy had apparently never encountered the shoulder-length variety of female hair. He wanted to know more. He poked at it and patted, and then grabbed a handful and yanked. He put a fistful in his mouth and made yummy sounds. Apparently dark brown hair with natural chestnut streaks was especially fascinating to this young man.

He leaned closer, his wide, watery blue eyes locked on her brown ones.

Then the plane made a sudden dip. The movement got a wail out of the little guy that went right through Liza's nerve endings. But at least he stopped chewing on her hair. Sleepy Mom roused at the noise, swinging the little guy back to her shoulder and patting him. "Sorry," she muttered, clearly too exhausted to say more.

*Me, too,* Liza thought, quietly checking her hair for any new additions or subtractions, courtesy of her young admirer.

The impromptu concert continued until the plane was almost on the ground at John Wayne Airport. By the time she stumbled her way from the Jetway into the airport gate area, Liza suspected she could have passed on the whole disguise thing. The under-three set were not the sort of people that would look at Liza and think *Hollywood!* And after that plane ride and her lack of sleep, she was sure she'd aged enough that no one from her former life would recognize her upon landing.

In the end, she stuck with the hat and sunglasses. They covered her hair and about half her face. She'd met a lot of people as a Hollywood publicist, and sometimes it seemed to Liza that you couldn't throw a stone in Southern California without hitting a movie person.

Liza sidestepped the general rush of the toddlers and their parents for the baggage-claim area. She'd brought everything she needed for the day in her carry-on. That left her free to chart a lone course along the airport's ground-floor concourse. Now her sunglasses seemed like a better idea, what with the bright light streaming in through the huge windows and bouncing off the vaulted ceiling high above. She headed for the main terminal entrance. Will Singleton, the sudoku maven who'd coaxed her down from her Northwest getaway for this tournament, was supposed to meet her at the statue of John Wayne.

After the noise, two-plus hours stuck on the flight, sleep deprivation, and, of course, her young admirer tugging on her hair, Liza shouldn't have been surprised at the ache pounding away in the space between her eyes. She wanted an aspirin and a nap — in

15

that order. At least Liza knew she could use some quiet time before tackling the sudoku tournament's qualification round. She'd need it. Will was famed for his tricky number puzzles. She fully intended to bring a prizewinner's trophy back with her on the evening's flight home.

In between? She smiled, despite the weight dragging at her shoulder. She had a good book and a blank notebook, and she'd probably have enough downtime to use them both. Liza shrugged the strap of her carry-on bag to a more comfortable position. It was heavier than usual. She had all her essentials handy, including a change of clothes and a kit if she decided to stay overnight.

At last Liza reached the nine-foot bronze memorial to Hollywood's biggest cowboy. She slowly turned, glancing around for Will or one of his minions when a pair of hands descended over her eyes.

Uh-oh.

This wasn't Will. For one thing, he'd have to reach *up* to try that trick on Liza. Besides, neither he nor any of the tournament staff knew her at all well enough to try anything like this.

Above all, she had played enough peekaboo this morning as it was.

The instincts of a childhood spent with a big brother who lived to pick on her, honed in adulthood by expensive Hollywood self-defense classes, kicked in. A sharp backward jab from Liza's elbow brought a gasp from her accoster. Her hands rose, easily brushing away his loosened grip. Her bag dropped to the floor as she swung round, fists in position to finish him off — then she froze.

She recognized her victim.

"Derrick?"

Derrick Robbins stood in a half crouch, both hands over his solar plexus, his handsome face twisted in pain as he tried to breathe. His complexion was a bit too red, then a bit too white, as the blow did what it was designed to do. It had knocked all the air out of his lungs for a moment.

Derrick's arms wildly semaphored for a second as he struggled for breath. His forehead unknotted and his color got better. But he had to suck in a little more air before he was able to make his reply.

"You know, the same thing happened when I tried that trick on a stunt woman who worked on my show," he finally wheezed. "I just didn't expect a knockout punch from a publicist."

"Soon to be *former* publicist," Liza reminded him. "Count yourself lucky. Michelle Markson would probably be carving trophies off you by now. You'd be ahead of the game if you still had both ears. Or perhaps she'd be looking elsewhere for her pound of flesh . . ."

Derrick shuddered at the mention of Liza's former partner, and possibly at the thought of her likely retribution. "It's unlucky to speak of the undead — whether you speak well or ill."

Liza had to stifle a smile at the actor's reaction. Her boss, Michelle Markson, had established herself as the female warlord of Hollywood publicity. Phrases like "hard-charging" and "take no prisoners" tended to crop up in descriptions of her style of doing business. With her media savvy and connections, Michelle could build a Hollywood career — or wreck it — with one well-planted blind item.

Working with Michelle had been good for Liza. She'd learned a great deal, had gained the skills to make her way in Tinseltown, had risen to the position of partner, but she had also earned the reputation as the human face of the partnership. People liked Liza — probably because Liza liked people. Perhaps the greatest proof of her people skills was the way she'd remained on good terms with Michelle even when she'd pulled up stakes, leaving the Hollywood rat race to return home to Maiden's Bay up in Oregon. When her life had turned upside down, Liza had opted for a less-stressful place to live out her next few years.

Right now, Derrick was looking like he wanted to send her back there.

The star gingerly rubbed his stomach. "That blow strikes me as a bit of overkill."

"Overreaction, maybe," Liza admitted. "I'm a bit on edge lately. I've got — well, I don't know what to call him. Stalker is a bit too harsh. Persistent, geeky hanger-on is too mild. Secret admirer is all wrong — I can't take a step without running into him. Anyway, he's starting to get on my nerves. I've been working this freelance gig up in Oregon, and I started the same day as this young computer tech. We went out for a new-kids lunch a few times, but now he's decided it's love, or fate, or something. He can't keep his eyes off me."

"Oh," Derrick said. "My."

"Yeah, exactly." She sighed. "I'm trying to figure out how to discourage him without hurting him."

"That jab in the gut hurt plenty, just so you know," Derrick said.

"Sorry about that." Liza grinned at her victim. "Announce yourself next time, and you'll get a more appropriate welcome. When you decided to go for the element of surprise, you made me think you might be Hank . . . and you know what happened. See, lately, he's been nerving himself up to try a PDA."

"A Public Display of Affection, eh?" Derrick said. "Why are you being so gentle with him — why? He sounds downright stalker-ish to me."

"I don't think he's trying to be a stalker. It's more like he's got a case of stunning social ineptitude. I'm afraid Hank veers between the silly stuff you'd expect to see in junior high and the kind of insane grand gestures he's read about in relationship books. He sent me a candygram the other day to celebrate national 'Be a Pal Day.' I've never heard of such a holiday, and I didn't even know they still sold candygrams."

"Hmm, I begin to see what was behind Liza's Dreaded Elbow of Death," Derrick said. "Not to mention why you'd prefer to take a relaxing break in sunny Orange County doing sudoku than staying holed up in your coastal paradise."

"And how do you know what I'm doing here?" Liza asked.

His sky blue eyes met hers with a cat-who-ate-the-canary twinkle. "Will Singleton is stuck handling some last-minute logistics for the tournament, so he asked me to pick you up. Your cover's blown, Liza K."

For a second, Liza stood openmouthed. Derrick's casual comment had done as effective a job of robbing her of words — and air — as her elbow had done on him.

*Omigod!* she thought. *He knows about Liza K! He knows everything!*

Liza K was the name she'd been using in her other life — her new life, as she preferred to call it. The dissolution of her marriage and her disillusion with the movie business had sent her back to her hometown. Coming to Maiden's Bay, she'd discovered real life, real people . . . and a real problem: earning a living.

Luckily, Liza also had some real friends, people she'd known since childhood. One of them was Ava Barnes, who'd gone into journalism and emerged as the managing editor of the *Oregon Daily.* She knew Liza was a sudoku whiz, and Ava also knew that more and more readers were playing the numbers game. She'd offered Liza a paying gig as the paper's resident sudoku expert, creating puzzles and writing a column with tips on finding solutions. The results had been better than Liza had dreamed. Now she faced the likelihood of national syndication and a revenue stream that would let her really leave Markson Associates behind.

Liza had long ago realized that Hollywood was a place that preferred car chases to certain intellectual pursuits. Which was fine, as far as it went, for most of Tinseltown. Film people loved to make fun of Bill Gates and the other technonerds up in Seattle and Redmond. So her ability with numbers and logic put Liza's credibility with the whole movie community at risk. Hollywood was famous for its disdain for bright women who didn't camouflage their intellectual abilities in public.

If the movers and shakers in The Business discovered that one of their top spinmeistresses was a closet übergeek up in Oregon, it would clash with the glamour of the world's film capital. Celebrities, fashion stars, and studio heads wanted their advisors to be smart, of course, but sudoku was the wrong kind of smart.

In fact, it was up there with braces, thick glasses, and a PhD as a Hollywood buzzkill.

And now, after keeping her sudoku life a secret for so long, this former television star was talking to her as if it were common knowledge.

Derrick Robbins responded to her look of shock with a grin that made him look like an oversized leprechaun. "Hey, maybe I only played a spy on TV, but still, ve haff vays . . ."

He relented, laughing. "Liza, I've been a sudoku junkie for years now. Maybe it was all those seasons as a cryptographer on *Spy-craft,* but I really got into codes and puzzles. Long before it was popular in the States, I'd have sudoku imported from the British papers and from Japan. And let's face it, the American sudoku world is still pretty small. I began to have suspicions when an Oregon paper started featuring a Liza K who wrote about sudoku right after you moved up there. Then I read your work, and I knew. You write like you talk — charmingly. Your secret was mine."

Derrick shrugged. "Of course, having Will ask me to pick you up kind of blew things wide open." He grinned again. "I was delighted to learn you'd be here. But I warn you now" — his grin broadened — "I'm here to win."

Liza smiled right back at him. "So am I."

# 2

Derrick picked up Liza's bag, which had flown to the foot of the pedestal supporting John Wayne's statue. He glanced up at the statue's bronze features. "You know, the Duke essentially played himself for something like fifty years." The actor shook his head as he offered the bag to Liza.

Liza understood. Derrick's career had started when he was a teenager, playing beautiful but troubled boys on the cusp of manhood. Then he'd gone on to play beautiful but troubled young men. The camera loved him, but in an unusual way. Liza had seen studios test thousands of ordinary-looking (usually extremely skinny) people to find the tiny minority that appeared beautiful on the screen. In real life, Derrick was a handsome guy with a bit of the leprechaun to him. But somehow, the camera made his features seem more delicate — more vulnerable.

That had worked against Derrick as he grew older. In Hollywood, beautiful, troubled people in midlife stayed strictly behind the cameras — usually in rehab. But he'd come back in a big way as the beautiful but quirkily brilliant cryptographer on *Spycraft.* The series had run for eight seasons, and Derrick's oddball character had moved from the background to become one of the show's stalwart stars. The producers had gone through two supposed female leads and one male one. None of them could outshine Derrick. By season four, Derrick and the black woman who played the tough-as-nails spymaster ended up with top billing and the highest pay.

Markson Associates had been brought in to boost the climactic final season, and Liza had been struck by the way Derrick managed to blend total professionalism with fun. Since *Spycraft* had wrapped last year, though, she hadn't heard much about Derrick — a bad sign. "What kind of scripts are you getting?" she asked as she settled her bag on her shoulder.

"Apparently, the world has decided that it's time for me to go against type. I'm being asked to play villains, psychos, and sickos. A spy movie, a couple of murder mysteries, and a lot of horror flicks." Derrick shook his head and shuddered theatrically. "I do *not* intend to become my generation's Tony Perkins."

That was enough to end that discussion. They headed outside, and Derrick led the way to the passenger loading area. "How was your flight?"

"Crowded and loud. Over a hundred kids yelling about visiting with a talking mouse and complaining about their inner ears." Liza couldn't help her rueful smile. "And there was a charming young man sitting next to me. Pity he was a few decades too young, had only four teeth, and drooled. But he was quite the flirt despite the handicap. I almost lost my heart to him — not to mention a good bit of my hair. I'm still fighting the pain of flying at thirty thousand feet and one hundred and sixty decibels." She paused to rub her forehead, hoping it would soothe the remnant of her headache away. While she massaged her brow, she looked around and spotted their target. "Nice car. Do you live in the area? Is it yours?"

"Nah. Will and Company arranged the limo," Derrick said. "I'm still up in Santa Barbara. Came down on my private jet."

"Of course you did," Liza muttered. "Doesn't everybody?"

Derrick's response was diplomatic. "Well, you'll have some time to recover. You're in the third round of the tournament. I'm in the first." He gave her another Cheshire-cat grin. "I'm glad you'll have the downtime. I want you in your best form before I take you out in the finals."

Liza wasn't sure whether to be amused or annoyed at his confidence that they would both meet in the final round.

Of course, she could hardly take offense when she felt the same way.

The driver of the car was alert, standing by the open door of the black Mercedes. Liza surrendered her bag and allowed herself to be handed inside. Back home, she'd have walked the distance to the airport hotel. Still, she couldn't complain about a little pampering and she had always enjoyed Derrick Robbins's droll conversation.

The Irvine Skytrails Hotel was large and fairly utilitarian except for some cast concrete flourishes and a large amount of greenery. It was part of a chain that could be found around airports all over the country — not the top of the line but not the bottom, either.

The heavy plate-glass door swung open, held by a uniformed staff member, and Derrick ushered Liza in. The lobby was surprisingly full. A glance around showed Liza that she was in the middle of Sudoku Nation. There was a woman of retirement age in a "nice" set of sweats by the front door, working on a practice puzzle. Moving past that person, she saw a middle-aged guy in a pair of seersucker slacks — surviving leftovers from an old suit. The man also wore a slightly frayed dress shirt and worn wingtip shoes. Obviously, this was a businessman trying to go casual. Equally obviously, he held to the thirty-year rule when it came to wingtips — ten years for work, ten for casual wear, five years as gardening shoes, and the remainder as a toy for the dog.

There was a gaggle of serious college students, complete with backpacks, trendy jeans, and what Liza called a "computer screen tan" — that pale, pale skin that was a product of never getting outside during daylight hours.

Smiling, Liza caught sight of another sudoku archetype actually reading a book on the subject — *The Complete Nincompoop's Guide to Sudoku.* This was a young guy in a pair of high-water chino pants and a faded T-shirt — a second-generation computer geek. (The first generation wore polyester shirts in colors that never existed in nature.)

She was still smiling as the guy put down his book. Then she stared at his too familiar face. "Hank?"

Hank Lonebaugh was the new computer guy at the *Oregon Daily* — the not-quite-stalker Liza had described to Derrick.

Glancing at her companion, she decided not to go on with the next logical question, which threatened to come out something like, "What the hell are you doing here, geek boy?"

Actually, Hank answered it without even being asked. "I was down visiting an old college bud, and heard about the tournament on the radio. Thought I'd come over and try it out. I am interested in sudoku, after all." He was trying to sound offhand, but came off nervous, almost defiant.

Oh yes, Hank had indeed developed an interest in sudoku after learning about Liza's column. But terms like "conjugate cells," "algorithms," and "recursion" kept cropping up in his discussions of the subject. Liza understood the mathematical and logical underpinnings for sudoku, but Hank always made it sound as if he were discussing the trajectory for sending a rocket to Mars when he talked about the subject. Liza had an entirely different approach to the puzzles. Shouldn't sudoku be fun?

Hank took a moment to direct a jealous glare at the man standing beside Liza. It was clear that Hank didn't like the idea of her with another man — especially one as compelling as Derrick. Then his eyes went wide with recognition. "Wait a minute! You're Derrick Robbins!"

*Of course,* Liza thought. *After his role on* Spycraft, *Derrick's the patron saint of geekdom.*

Caught between jealousy, frustrated love, and hero worship, Hank veered away from Liza like an iron filing attracted by a very strong magnet — Derrick. He stuck out his hand.

Derrick shook it.

"You were the coolest thing on *Spycraft*!" Hank said breathlessly.

With a wry smile and a wink for Liza delivered behind Hank's back, Derrick led Hank away. They'd actually gotten a dozen feet from Liza before Hank belatedly looked back over his shoulder at her. "We're both in the third round — I'll talk with you then!"

*Not if I can help it,* Liza thought.

She turned away, very thankful indeed to Derrick for running interference, and saw Will Singleton rushing across the lobby. The little man was making an effort to be calm as he led Liza to a private lounge. "This place makes its money from business travelers, mainly during the Monday through Friday rush. I figured they'd be happy to get some bodies in here over the weekend. But it looks like they're a little discombobulated."

Liza saw what he meant when she glanced around at the table featuring neat pyramids of soda, juice, and bottled water . . . but apparently, no ice. Will caught the look and collared one of his minions to get a supply. "I've tried calling the kitchen. No response so far. Go upstairs and hit the ice machines in each floor if you have to," he ordered. The sudoku guru's decisive tone evaporated as he turned to his guest of honor. "Looks like we're going to be roughing it a bit. But I'm going to make it work."

Soon enough, Liza was ensconced in the most comfortable chair available, her eyes closed and a glass of iced water in her hand. *Maybe I should have come down yesterday,* she told herself. *Will did offer me a room.* But that would have meant leaving Rusty in a kennel, or imposing on some friend to dogsit.

Barely a week after returning to Maiden's Bay, she'd encountered a mutt wandering the neighborhood and ended up rescuing

31

him from the local animal control unit. Judging from the reddish cast of his coat, Rusty had some Irish setter in his background, but he didn't have that breed's high-strung temperament. Still, he hated to be left alone, and Liza had suffered surprising regret at leaving him. She'd never been so attached to anyone that a day's absence worried her like this.

*Keep this up, and I'll be adding a herd of cats and a shawl to the mix,* Liza told herself. *I've already got the rocking chair.* She was supposed to be establishing a new life for herself, not becoming an eccentric hermit. Maybe this tournament was just what she needed, an opportunity to get out in the world, see people, and do something she enjoyed.

She smiled to herself. If that meant dealing with Hank Lovelorn, so be it. And if Derrick Robbins wanted a contest, he'd get one. Bring on the sudoku!

Most of the crowd in the lobby boiled through the double doors when they opened. A brass plaque announced the space was the Irvine Room. Old-line hotels would have called it the ballroom. In modern hotelspeak, it was an event room. Liza had used about a million of them in her career as a publicist, as venues for major announcements, project launches, or Q-and-A sessions. This particular space was probably aimed more at business events, sales conferences, or maybe high-end computer fairs.

She ran a professional's eyes over the room as she stepped inside. Commercial carpet, about five years old from the pattern — due to be replaced soon. Four sets of accordion-style partitions, all of them retracted into the walls. Pillars set against the walls in the Skytrails Hotel chain colors, not for any load-bearing function but to break up what would otherwise be a big, beige box.

Right now the box was filled with an array of long tables, but these weren't set for dining. The tablecloths in the corporate colors were decorated with widely spaced settings of pads and pencils, and the rows of matching chairs were set in a staggered pattern. It looked like a very upscale setup for a standardized test. Liza's lips twisted in a wry smile — SATs 90210.

As she trailed behind the main body of contestants, Hank Lonebaugh kept rushing toward the door, then coming back to her. His back-and-forth moves reminded Liza of Rusty trying to get her to take him for a walk. Since he'd found her again, Hank had indeed talked to her. Mostly, though, the conversation had been along the lines of, "You never said that Derrick Robbins was your friend. He's a really cool guy — very nice, too. Don't you think he's a cool, nice guy?" It made for a pleasant break from what Hank usually talked about.

It seemed Derrick had made quite an impression on poor Hank.

They came through the door, and things worked out exactly as Liza expected. She didn't need to rush in to find a seat. Will Singleton had reserved spots for his honored guests. Liza snorted when she saw he'd placed her right up front.

Hank had gestured to a seat next to him, but Liza was able to point to the head table and gently detach herself. She left Hank behind in a rear row while she took her seat in the front of the room facing the dais.

As the crowd settled at the various tables, Will stood up. "This is our third elimination round of five," he began. "Each participant in this round will receive the same sudoku puzzle and have the same time of forty-five minutes to complete it." He gestured at the large digital display on the front table, already set at 45:00.

*Just the thing to make any nervous players*

*completely crazy,* Liza thought. *Did somebody donate that monstrosity? It doesn't seem like a Will Singleton touch.*

"The first five people to turn in a correct solution will advance to the final round," Will went on. "Is everyone ready?"

As Will's minions began dropping off sealed manila envelopes containing the puzzle, Liza took a moment to reexamine the points on her pencils and made sure both of her pens wrote correctly. That was the only equipment contestants were allowed to have on their tabletops.

Liza turned at the sounds of a commotion behind her. A young woman, one of the people giving out the puzzles, was taking something out of Hank's hand. "I'm sorry, sir, but those aren't allowed."

It was a handheld sudoku solver. "B-but how am I supposed to figure all the candidates — ?"

"Like everybody else — by hand," Will cut in. From his tone of voice, somebody had done the same thing in the two previous rounds. "Any technological help, be it handheld sudoku solvers, Black-Berries, or even cell phones, has been banned."

The young woman brought the handheld device up to Will, who stuck it on the table

35

behind him. "You can retrieve this after this round."

"But —" Hank said in a forlorn voice, reaching out after his technological crutch.

"The rules are quite explicit, and they appeared on the contest form that you signed." Looking every inch the sudoku guru, Singleton glanced around the room. He projected a surprising amount of dignity for his small stature. The envelopes had all been distributed. Liza took a deep breath as Will reached over to the display. "All right then. Sudoku!"

Along with every other contestant in the room, she tore open the envelope to reveal an oversized square grid, nine by nine — eighty-one spaces in all. Some of the spaces

| 7 |   |   |   |   | 3 |   |   |   |
|---|---|---|---|---|---|---|---|---|
| 2 | 4 |   |   | 8 |   |   |   |   |
|   | 8 |   | 5 | 4 |   |   |   | 7 |
| 3 |   |   |   | 1 | 7 |   |   |   |
|   | 2 |   | 6 |   | 4 |   | 3 |   |
|   |   | 6 | 7 |   |   |   |   | 8 |
| 4 |   |   |   | 1 | 2 |   | 7 |   |
|   |   |   |   | 7 |   |   | 6 | 4 |
|   |   |   | 4 |   |   |   |   | 2 |

were filled with numbers, the givens or clues. The rest of the spaces were blank, up to her to fill in.

The rules were simple. Each of the nine rows right to left, each of the columns top to bottom, and each of the nine three-by-three boxes that made up the gridwork must hold the numbers one through nine. Based on the given numbers, Liza had to figure out the one and only solution that fit the pattern. Some people called sudoku a "numbers crossword" or a math puzzle. But there was no number crunching involved. This was an exercise in pure logic.

Liza began to scan the entire puzzle. *Look at the forest, not the trees,* she told herself, running her eyes over the sets of boxes, both

| 7 |   |   |   | 3 |   |   |   |   |
|---|---|---|---|---|---|---|---|---|
| 2 | 4 |   |   | 8 | 7 |   |   |   |
|   | 8 |   | 5 | 4 |   |   |   | 7 |
| 3 |   |   |   |   | 1 | 7 |   |   |
|   | 2 |   | 6 |   | 4 |   | 3 |   |
|   |   | 6 | 7 |   |   |   |   | 8 |
| 4 |   |   |   | 1 | 2 |   | 7 |   |
|   |   |   |   | 7 |   |   | 6 | 4 |
|   |   |   | 4 |   |   |   |   | 2 |

across and down.

It was hard to miss the combination of 7s in the top tier of boxes. These numbers appeared in the first row of the first box and in the third row of the third box. That meant there had to be a 7 in the middle row of the middle box. Only two of the three spaces were available — an 8 occupied the center space. Four spaces down from the left-hand space was a 7, eliminating that open cell as a candidate. So there was only one solution. Liza picked up her pen and entered a 7 to the puzzle.

The second tier of boxes also had two spaces occupied by 7s. From their placement (and the fact that there was a 7 in the first vertical column), that meant a 7 could

| 7 |   |   |   |   | 3 |   |   |   |
| 2 | 4 |   |   | 8 | 7 |   |   |   |
|   | 8 |   | 5 | 4 |   |   |   | 7 |
| 3 |   |   |   | 1 | 7 |   |   |   |
|   | 2 | 7 | 6 |   | 4 |   | 3 |   |
|   |   | 6 | 7 |   |   |   |   | 8 |
| 4 |   |   |   | 1 | 2 |   | 7 |   |
|   |   |   |   | 7 |   |   | 6 | 4 |
|   |   | 7 |   | 4 |   |   |   | 2 |

only appear in the right-hand space on the middle row of the left center box. Checking the bottom tier, Liza cross-checked the rows and columns and found that the existing 7s ruled out all the spaces in the bottom row except for one. She quickly penned 7 in that remaining box.

*Three down, forty-something to go,* Liza thought as she found another cue in the lower tier of boxes. The number 2 appeared in the first row across and the third. Cross-checking the columns for the available spaces forced another solution.

Soon enough, however, she'd found all the obvious matchups. Then her pencil came into play, listing the possible candidate numbers to fill each empty space. It became a process of elimination, zooming in to cross-check spaces with the least numbers of candidates, then zooming out to see how each solution affected the puzzle as a whole. Each time she placed a number in ink, the circle of unknowns shrank.

Liza frowned. She was moving right along — too fast, in fact. What was Will up to with this puzzle? She found herself solving it with the simplest techniques in her arsenal — the kind of stuff that Hank was reading in his Nincompoops sudoku book. Easy logic quickly uncovered some candidates — and just as quickly eliminated others. Where were the really tricky moves — the X-wing solutions depending on four spaces at once, the Swordfish configurations that rested on six?

*If Will had a real brain-buster up his sleeve, it should have shown by now,* Liza thought worriedly. *I'm running out of spaces with candidates.*

But no last-minute brilliance in puzzle development appeared. The number of spaces with more than one candidate kept contracting, right down to a final set of solutions.

Liza took a long, deep breath, almost a snort. Maybe it was too easy, but it was a definite solution. She pushed all niggling doubts aside and began checking for any errors. Her focus was now entirely on the sheet of paper before her. The digital display and the murmurs from the proctors and onlookers receded from her consciousness.

But Liza came back to the world with a thump — an audible thump, she suddenly realized. Liza looked over her shoulder to see Hank, his face shining, sitting up straight and holding out his puzzle. One of the proctors took the paper and brought it up to Will. After studying it for a moment, he shook his head. "I'm sorry, this is not correct."

Hank's face crumpled. "I — I —" He rose from his seat and slunk from the Irvine Room, blinking back tears.

*Probably didn't double-check* his *solution,* Liza thought as she began that very process on her puzzle. A painstaking recap through every space in each row, column, and box could take minutes. But it could also avoid a careless — and disastrous — mistake. Liza looked down at her solution. It was ready.

Silently, she turned her puzzle sheet over. A proctor instantly whisked it away. Will Singleton perused it and smiled. "We have our first successful completion."

Liza blinked as her focus slowly expanded. The digital display had counted down barely a quarter of the allotted time.

# 3

Will Singleton gave Liza a nod as she rose from her seat and headed for the rear of the event room. Along the way, she was aware of several sets of eyes following her — a couple of them competitive, some nervously going from her to the clock up front. And one guy, she suspected, was checking out her butt.

*Concentrate on the puzzle, not the scenery,* she silently scolded all of them.

When she reached the double doors, a proctor opened them for her — another perk for the celebrity guest? She wondered.

Liza stepped out into the corridor, releasing a long-repressed sigh. But she cut that short when she saw Derrick Robbins leaning against the opposite wall. All he needed were a few feathers drifting past his mouth to underscore the cat-and-canary look on his face.

"Your . . . friend came out in a hurry,"

Derrick said. "I'm afraid he didn't look very successful. In fact, he muttered something about going home, then almost ran for the exit."

Liza gave a different kind of sigh. "I guess he found it hard to face me."

"I sincerely hope that's what kept you in there." Derrick made an elaborate production out of consulting his watch. "I've been waiting for several minutes more than I expected."

"Maybe you can talk to Will about where he got that monster clock sitting up beside him," Liza suggested. "Then I could see exactly how long you had to lean there."

"Time is of the essence when it comes to competitive sudoku," Derrick scolded her. "You never talk about that in your column."

"That's because most of my columns are about helping people who have just started with sudoku," Liza tartly replied. She gave him a sharp look. "You really read what I write?"

"Religiously." Derrick put a hand to his chest and gave her a beatific smile. Then he got serious again. "I like your stuff. But I think you don't always go far enough into the game. There are enough sudoku players to get into the tough stuff every once in a while. And you're very methodical. You talk a lot about pencil work, listing all the possibilities for each and every box. If you did that for your contest round, I'm surprised you're out by now."

"It's a fundamental," Liza said. "The people who read my column have to learn to walk before they can skate."

"Maybe, but it makes things a bit boring for people like me," Derrick complained. "Can't you occasionally discuss techniques like Swordfish or Nishio?"

"I suspect that a reader like you is one in a million." Liza laughed. "And I don't have a million readers yet." She turned a speculative eye at Derrick. "Would you be willing to discuss your methods for publication? We could do a series of columns . . ."

Derrick's expressive features took on a look of excessive modesty. "I don't know. As you say, a lot of it goes to having a cultivated eye." He shot her a quick look. "The rest might make heavy going for beginners. I will admit to one quirk, though. I like to solve my puzzles in numerical order."

Liza gave him a sharp glance. Was Derrick just being outrageous, or was this a competitor's attempt at psychological warfare?

Derrick certainly talked a good game. On the other hand, some people considered the

Nishio technique to be little better than guesswork. Liza decided to find out how well he'd placed in his group as soon as she got away.

That wasn't going to be soon, it seemed. "If you're recovered enough, how about some lunch?" Derrick asked.

Liza was happy to say yes.

They ate on a shaded terrace facing away from the airport. Liza poked an appreciative fork at her *frutti di mare* salad. "Will really outdid himself on the catering —"

She faltered as Derrick ducked his head like an abashed kid. "I happen to know a guy with a little restaurant down in Newport. And the hotel management was agreeable."

"I should have expected something was up, since we're the only ones out here."

Derrick shrugged. "Sometimes the TV-star thing can smooth the way for me." His grin was still boyish, until a closer look at his skin revealed the start of fine wrinkles.

Something of that shock must have shown on her face, because Derrick's grin grew lopsided. "Give me ten years, and I should be able to pull a Leif Erickson."

"The Viking?" Liza asked in puzzlement.

"No, the actor." Derrick replied. "As a young man, he got typecast as a pretty boy.

When he got older, his pretty face got rugged and craggy, and he had a whole second act as an authority figure."

"I see." Liza cocked her head. "And what exactly will you do to prepare for your second act?"

"Practice my squint, smile a lot, and avoid Botox like the plague."

That got a laugh from her. "And what will you be doing during the intermission between acts?"

Derrick got more serious. "Hopefully, some directing. I did a few episodes all through the last few seasons of *Spycraft*, and I've gotten some bites. Also, there's a project I want to produce." Now he became mysterious. "In fact, I've got some footage I'd like you to see."

"Is the wide-screen monitor coming up out of the shrubbery, or do we go to a private screening room?" Liza joked.

"Option B — but it's a long ride."

She glanced at her watch. "How far? Is there time?"

"It's in Santa Barbara, in my house," Derrick admitted. He quickly raised a hand to cut off her protests. "I've got a plane, remember. We can offer you dinner —"

"You know I'm trying to get out of the PR business," Liza began.

"I understand," Derrick replied. "But you know I'm never going to get anywhere near Michelle. At best, she considers me last year's model — or is that last decade's?" He made a visible effort to cool off. "Maybe it wasn't a good idea, ambushing you like this. But I don't want some shlub assistant looking at this."

"Well, since the ambush included a good lunch, I'll make you a sporting proposition," Liza said. "Whoever comes in with the higher score makes the decision. How's that?"

"You're on," Derrick said.

At the end of lunch, Liza headed for the ladies' room. She knew it wasn't easy to solve any kind of puzzle with bladder pressure disrupting concentration. She also took a moment to check out the posted results. Derrick had come in number one for his group.

"So, I guess it's a sporting proposition after all," she muttered as she headed back to the event room. Inside, there were now only twenty-five spaces for the competitors. Will tried to place her right beside Derrick, but Liza shook her head. She accepted a seat in the first row, but on the other end from the actor.

It wasn't just her desire to keep a low

profile that had her sitting as far away from Derrick as she could get. Knowing Derrick's prankish nature, it was better not to give him any temptation. And after she opened the envelope for the final competition, Liza was sure she'd made the right decision. Will might not have had a hand in the catering for their terrace lunch, but he'd certainly outdone himself on this puzzle. Liza soon found herself abandoning her pen and sketching possibilities in with her pencil. Row by row, column by column, box by box. *Ah. Out of the nine spaces in this box, only one has a 3. Get the pen.*

Her eyes skittered around the puzzle, but not at random. When it came to sudoku, much of the battle was won by observation. Here was a space with only two possibilities, a 1 and a 4, and farther down the column another space with the same pair as the only possibilities. Some sudoku aficionados called numbers like these naked pairs. One of those two numbers definitely went in one of those two spaces, so Liza could eliminate 1 and 4 from every other space in the column. Naked pairs could also be found in rows or squares, too. With experience, Liza had learned to spot naked triplets and even quadruplets. Each one she discov-

48

ered eliminated possibilities from other spaces.

A trained eye like Liza's could also detect hidden pairs, matching numbers hidden among lists of four, five, or six possibilities. Again, each discovery eliminated possible numbers in other squares, reducing the circle of uncertainty.

The world receded as Liza's eyes and brain roved the eighty-one little squares. Will had designed this puzzle with experts in mind, and Liza soon had to dig deeper into her bag of tricks, using more exotic techniques, shaving away the possibilities until only one logical choice remained for each space.

She heard a slight disturbance while she checked over her solution but only covered her ears, concentrating on the puzzle. Yes. Done.

Liza turned over her paper. A glance at the clock showed she'd taken a good twenty minutes longer on this puzzle. Then she looked at Will, who gave her a congratulatory nod — but with an odd expression on his face. She discovered why when she turned to leave.

Politely holding the door for her was Derrick Robbins.

The road from the private airfield quickly began to rise into the mountains surrounding Santa Barbara. Derrick drove the car, a nondescript SUV, just as expertly as he'd piloted the plane up from Orange County. "I hope you're not expecting John Travolta Airlines," he'd said when he conducted her across the tarmac to a small Learjet. "I don't own a fleet of 747s."

"This is beautiful. And you can't beat the view." Since she had the seat next to the pilot, the flight had been an amazing visual treat. Southern California had rolled beneath them in all its splendor on the short flight.

Liza had decided to share the cockpit with him rather than sit in the small but luxurious passenger compartment. She wanted to see where they were going, even if they were going to crash.

Thankfully, Derrick turned out to be as good at piloting as he was at sudoku. And that was very good indeed. In the end, less than a minute separated their solving times for both puzzles. Liza realized that the small commotion she'd blocked out must have been Derrick turning in his solution. "If I hadn't gone over that puzzle one more time . . ." she began.

"You wouldn't have been Liza K," Derrick finished for her. He'd been a very good winner, not insisting on making her honor their bet, which somehow had made Liza feel even more obligated to go with him to Santa Barbara. After a call to Mrs. Halvorsen, her next-door neighbor, to ensure that Rusty would be taken care of, Liza had shouldered her bag and accompanied Derrick to the general aviation section of John Wayne Airport — the part serving small planes.

"What were you sweet-talking Will Singleton for before we left?" Derrick asked as they boarded his plane.

"I merely agreed to return Hank Lonebaugh's sudoku solver. It's a fairly expensive model —"

" 'Agreed,' huh?" Derrick squinted over at her. "That's a Michelle Markson word. Most people would offer to help out. *Agreed* suggests an exchange of favors."

Liza shrugged. "Well, he did give me a copy of the puzzle he unleashed on us — and the one from the entry round you were in."

"Of course," Derrick said, "he'd need different puzzles for each round, to discourage

51

collusion or cheating."

"I've certainly never tried to memorize a sudoku," Liza said. "Anyway, I'm going to use both of them in my column to discuss techniques for dealing with easy and tough puzzles."

"I'm surprised you didn't fold them up and put them in your bra." Derrick glanced over again. "Which I wouldn't advise. It would ruin the lines —"

"Just keep your eyes on your driving — or flying, or whatever," Liza told him.

And Derrick had. The cockpit view for their flight up the California coast had been interesting, stretches of emerald green (representing carefully watered lawns) cropping up against the reddish brown, arid tones of the natural landscape where development had yet to extend its tentacles.

Now, looking out the SUV's window, she found plenty of growth on the rocky slopes around them, mainly of the evergreen variety. Was the greenery natural or irrigated? Given the price of the real estate up here, she could well imagine hand-planted forests being installed to improve the view.

Derrick's place was a surprise, a somewhat rambling house of native stone tucked away on a flank of the rising slope. Liza could hardly make it out from the distance.

"You were expecting maybe a hacienda?" Derrick joked, glancing at her expression as he parked. "My dad was a salesman, and he hated the hot dogs who were always showing off. Brand-new cars, brand-new suits, all bought on credit. I guess I picked up the same attitude, so when I had the chance, I built this place for comfort, not for show."

He hefted her travel bag. "Besides, with a small place, I can get by with just a couple people coming in by day to help out with the upkeep and cleaning. So don't expect a majordomo."

He conducted her inside, and Liza could see what he meant. The place wasn't palatial, but was definitely roomy, and whoever had done the décor hadn't left interior designer fingerprints over everything. The furniture was a surprise, amber-toned all-year wicker, somewhat on the rustic side, definitely masculine, and downright comfortable.

After allowing Liza a quick pit stop, Derrick brought her to what he called "the movie-star part of the house," a plush home theater that doubled as a private screening room.

"We'll get this done, then no more obligation," he said as he cued up the film. "It's just a scene — a screen test, really."

He shut up as an image appeared on the big screen — a clapper board with a scrawled name on it — J something or other.

Then a girl walked into camera range. *Oho,* Liza thought as the girl began a fairly tense scene with another actor. The young woman was beautiful, a commodity Liza had come to expect in Hollywood. But this was a beauty that translated well to the screen, or as insiders would say, "The camera loved her."

In fact, the young woman had a feminine version of Derrick's own screen attractiveness — a good brow, a straight nose with just a hint of uptilt, generous lips, and big green eyes that went perfectly with her russet hair. As evidenced by the brief scene, she moved gracefully, had some traces of acting training . . . and had to be about thirty years younger than Derrick.

The scene ended, and Liza turned to Derrick. "So you've found yourself a protégée?"

"She's my niece — no, really," he assured her. "I wouldn't be caught dead using such an old-fashioned Hollywood line. She's my older brother's only child. Jenny lost both parents in a car accident a couple years ago, and now she's come out here after finishing drama school."

Derrick looked at Liza — the perfect image of a defendant waiting for a verdict. "So am I crazy, or does she have it?"

"Well, you *are* crazy," Liza replied, unable to resist the straight line. "But I think you're right about Jenny."

Beautiful boys with talent often wound up with Hollywood careers like Derrick's — playing beautiful but troubled men until their beauty turned craggy. Beautiful girls with talent, however, provided they weren't completely brainless or complete witches, only had the trouble of picking between dozens of scripts. Jenny Robbins had what it took to go places, if she had the right backing. And Markson Associates could do that . . .

"I'll get in touch with Michelle and make sure the test gets to her," Liza promised as they exited the screening room. "I think once she sees —"

She broke off when she found a young woman hovering in the hallway outside — Jenny Robbins, in the flesh.

"What are you doing here?" Derrick asked in obvious surprise.

"I decided to drive up. It seemed kind of silly, waiting at home while you discussed . . . I mean, while the two of you . . ." The girl glanced from Derrick to Liza, color slowly rising in her face.

"I thought you were seeing Liza Kelly. Did I come on the wrong day? Am I in the way here? I can leave if this is supposed to be a . . . um, special evening or something."

Liza looked over at Derrick, who suddenly had a similar rush of color. For that matter, Liza's own cheeks felt warm. Well, it had been a possibility ever since she'd met Derrick at the airport. He was a widower, and she was well and truly separated from her husband. There had been a little spice of boy-girl in the way they'd gotten along since they'd "met cute."

"I'm Liza Kelly," she said, extending a hand. "I think that was a great audition, by the way — glad your uncle brought me up here to see it. We discussed the best accommodations for me on the drive up here," Liza said tactfully, mentioning the name of a fairly posh resort on the other side of town. Michelle had used it to put up people who were passing through Santa Barbara. "I plan to stay there tonight."

While Liza shook hands with a mortified Jenny, Derrick stood behind the girl, shooting Liza a grateful look.

"I'll get the number and make a reservation for you," he said, heading off to the phone.

Jenny swallowed audibly. "I'm sorry I

acted like such a geek." She had lived down most of her embarrassment but was still fairly nervous. Out of makeup, the girl had a sprinkle of freckles under her California tan.

"Uncle D never mentioned you were Asian. After hearing the name Liza Kelly, I guess I expected —"

"Something completely different," Liza finished for her. "I guess I'm a Hibernasian — Dad was Irish, and Mom's family came from Japan."

"Well, I think you got the best of both worlds," Jenny told her. "With looks like yours, I'm surprised you're not in front of the camera."

"I never even thought of that," Liza confessed, "which is a good thing. I don't translate well to the screen. With my figure, I look like Xena, so I'd have to live on a starvation diet for a traditional movie career. Which reminds me — what's for supper?"

"I stopped off at a farmer's market to get the makings of a good salad. Uncle D always has half a cow or something in the freezer —" She broke off, anxious again. "Unless you're a vegetarian. So many of you Hollywood types are." She paused, then realized her gaffe. "Not that there's anything wrong with that."

"Well, I think I could go for a quarter of a cow," Liza told her, "and I bet so could you. So Derrick will just have to fend for himself."

Jenny grinned, at ease again.

They dined alfresco in the rear of the house. A low wall topped with planters marked the end of the flagstone terrace. Beyond, they looked down and across the mountains to the sea in the distance. Jenny had brought an abundance of salad and expertly grilled a few steaks.

Derrick reappeared wearing a shabby sweater with a pattern loud enough to make Liza wince. "They've got a nice room ready for you," he said. "And I dug up a bottle of the good merlot." He blew dust off the bottle while his other hand juggled three long-stemmed, wide-belled wineglasses.

"Why don't you just wipe it with that rag you're wearing?" Liza kidded.

"My lucky sweater?" Derrick replied, shocked. "I've had it for years — I even thought of wearing it to the tournament. And you'd be glad for a sweater when this terrace gets a bit cooler."

"Give me that one and I'll throw it over the side," Liza mock-threatened while Derrick expertly removed the cork to let the wine breathe. He poured out the heady red wine as his niece began serving their meal. Jenny picked up her glass and sipped appreciatively, a good sign in Liza's book. She never trusted that white-wine crowd. In fact, after settling down and getting into safer conversation, Jenny pretty much confirmed Liza's impression of her as a nice kid, if a little anxious right now.

Seeing that things were going well, Derrick had settled down, too, keeping up an interesting flow of table talk. "Like it or not, the acting business is about looks, and you've got those," he told Jenny. "For the rest, all you have to do is remember your lines and not bump into the scenery."

"You stole that from Laurence Olivier," Jenny accused her uncle impishly.

"The world's greatest actor," Derrick replied. "I bet he also said to steal from the best."

Jenny got embarrassed again when she heard how her uncle had gotten Liza to the house in the first place.

By now, though, Liza had gotten philosophical about coming in second at the sudoku tournament. *A* close *second,* she reminded herself. "Looking at it from a publicity viewpoint, Will probably likes it better that Derrick won instead of Liza K."

"You've got a point there," Derrick admitted. "Liza K is somebody the sudoku mavens know. But Will can probably get a lot more mileage with the general public with an actor, even with a has-been actor like me."

"You're not a has-been," Jenny loyally argued. "And you'd know how popular you still are if you didn't lock yourself up in your study."

"Locking myself in my study is how I won the championship today," he replied. "You'd be amazed at what you can find sometimes in sudoku."

Derrick turned to Liza. "Do you follow the puzzles in the *Seattle Prospect*?"

"I've tried a few," Liza admitted, "but not since I started working for the *Oregon Daily*. The folks on my paper consider the *Prospect* to be their deadly enemy."

"Well, I've got a daily subscription for both. I enjoy your column, but I'm intrigued by the *Prospect*. And a bit worried. Whoever does the puzzles for them is a worse recluse than Liza K. I haven't been able to find out who the creators are, and I want to." He frowned. "And there's something strange about the *Prospect* columns. They're not just puzzles, they're codes."

Liza blinked. "Really?"

"I think whoever's behind those puzzles is

sending messages — and it's not anything innocuous like 'Happy Birthday.' " He looked down at the table, brooding. "I worry I'm getting paranoid. Then I look at the puzzles, and I know I'm not. I don't care how much they complained," he muttered. "They didn't deserve to be burned — and they sure as hell didn't get burnt with the Lord's fire."

For a long moment, Liza and Jenny stared, openmouthed, at Derrick, both at a loss for words. Had he suddenly flipped his lid? What on earth was he talking about? Liza wondered. Then Derrick looked up and went back to his normal charming self. "Enough of that. What have we got for dessert?"

Jenny hurried off to slice up some fruit and cheese, clearly relieved to leave the table. Derrick disappeared for a bottle of Essensia, leaving Liza to wonder if she'd imagined what had just happened.

Derrick returned, totally playing the role of considerate host. "You've got to try this," he said. "It's like liquid sunshine."

Liza stayed in her seat, staring off into the gathering dusk. *Just when I start to really like the guy, he brings out snapshots of his last visit to the Twilight Zone! What just happened here?*

The wine was excellent, a sweet muscat flavored with orange essence, perfectly complemented with chocolate biscotti. The fruit and cheese were great, too. But the conversation suffered after Derrick's lapse into strangeness, no matter how normal he seemed now. A pall of discomfort hung over the table, and conversation degenerated into compliments on the deliciousness of the repast.

"It's getting a bit late," Liza finally said, breaking into another round of trite observations about the food. "Maybe I should call a cab."

"That's a point. We've had enough wine that I probably shouldn't drive you myself." Derrick led Liza to the kitchen phone.

"Twenty minutes," she announced after talking with the dispatcher.

"Then you have time to see one thing." Derrick brought her down a hallway to a beautifully paneled door. "I think you'll really like it. The entrance to my study," he said with an ironic smile. "As you've heard, Jenny hates it when I hole up in here."

Liza almost had to catch her breath as she looked around. Built-in shelves held a library on sudoku and cryptography that any university or government agency would covet. A wide teak desk facing a window with the same view as the terrace provided a working space for Derrick. His desk was empty now except for a folded newspaper and one discordant note — a Gideon Bible, its leatherette cover faded and worn almost to tatters.

"Need religion to help you get through the hardest puzzles?" Liza teased.

Derrick glanced over at it. "It's a personal item — very sentimental. My dad was a traveling salesman. That Bible gave him a lot of comfort during some bad times on the road." He smiled reminiscently. "While my brother and I were growing up, Dad often quoted the Good Book to us, chapter and verse. When he passed on, I ended up with it."

The actor's smile faded. "Imagine my surprise when I fooled around with one of those oddball *Prospect* puzzles and found a reference to one of Dad's favorite taglines from his old Gideon Bible.

"I thought it was a fluke, but I decided to decode some copies of old *Prospect* puzzles I had around here. Not only did more quotes turn up, but I realized they tied in with stuff happening in the news — bad stuff."

He stopped when he saw the expression on Liza's face. "I know you're hoping I've got some kind of punch line coming up when I talk about this. I don't. I just know something funny's going on, and I don't like it. Unfortunately, this isn't a pitch for a flick called *Conspiracy Theory II*. I'm serious. Somebody on that paper is up to no good. I wanted to run this past someone who knows sudoku, and I was planning to do it at the tournament today. Unfortunately, Will was running around like a madman the whole time we were there and I never was able to get him alone, so you're elected. You're the first person I've spoken to, and I probably shouldn't have waited until we finished the second bottle of wine to do it."

"To me it seems like an unlikely place to send messages. Too public." Liza shrugged. "I certainly don't know what I could tell you that would shed any light on this. Are you sure this is really some kind of embedded coded message?"

"As for that, I took the bull by the horns." Derrick patted the old Bible. "I found a quote I thought was appropriate to what was going on, encoded it the same way the *Prospect*'s puzzle creator has been doing in a puzzle of my own, and sent it off to the *Prospect.* If I'm crazy, then nothing will happen. If I'm not crazy . . . well, we'll see. I thought I should mention it to somebody

— somebody who might understand. Like you."

He stepped away from the desk, suddenly businesslike. "So what's our next step with Jenny?"

"I'll talk to Michelle tonight — sound her out," Liza said, a bit relieved at the change of subject. "If we're lucky, she may fax me a contract. Or I may need a copy of Jenny's screen test from you as a convincer."

Derrick nodded. "Either way, stop up here tomorrow morning, and I'll either run you back to Portland or drop you at John Wayne for the commercial flight. Is seven thirty too early?"

"Sounds good to m—", Liza's reply was interrupted by a knock at the door.

Jenny popped her head inside. "The cab's here," she said.

Liza didn't know whether to be relieved or disappointed.

But she knew it was a good idea to think about all she'd heard tonight before she acted on it.

"Thanks," she said. "I'll get my bag and my hat."

# 4

Liza's hotel room boasted a good-sized balcony with a pleasant enough view. It didn't even come close to the vista from Derrick Robbins's terrace, though.

After stowing away the contents of her carry-on bag (a pretty quick job, really), Liza went out onto the balcony. Dropping into one of the chairs, she took out her cell phone and dialed Michelle Markson's home number.

Liza expected to get the answering machine, but got a live voice instead — Michelle greeting her brusquely. "What's up, Liza?"

Oh, the joys of caller ID.

"I was down in Orange County and bumped into Derrick Robbins —"

Michelle didn't go as far as interrupting Liza with her imitation of the harsh buzzer sound quiz shows use to greet wrong answers. But she did interrupt by cutting right over Liza's sentence, disinterest dripping from every word. "Derrick hasn't worked since *Spycraft* wrapped."

Translation: Derrick might as well have fallen off the edge of the world.

"He's been exploring the production end, and he showed me a screen test —"

"This town really does move fast. He can't impress the girls by being a star himself, so he's got to use the casting couch?" Michelle let out a long breath, a sign that she was really reaching the end of her patience. "I know you're supposed to be the nice partner. Huh. Well, you can tell Derrick you talked with me."

*I really have been out of the rat race too long,* Liza thought. *Even with Michelle, I've got to keep the pitch short and sweet.*

"This isn't about Derrick." She spoke quickly before Michelle hung up on her. "From what I saw of that screen test, we may be looking at the next Julia Roberts."

There was a long pause. Liza could just imagine her partner, finger poised halfway to disconnecting the call.

"Tell me more."

"She's Derrick's niece, and I'd say she got all the right family genes. She comes across on camera as well as he did when he was a kid, and the look works better for her."

"Mmm-hmm."

"The camera loves her. She has great presence and moves well — just out of drama school, so she's got some student-actor issues. Not a problem with a good director to give her the basics on film work as opposed to stage acting. I've even met her, and she strikes me as a nice kid. Jenny Robbins has all the raw talent anyone could want. She just needs polishing."

"Mmm. So you decided to call me with this little gift as your going-away present for leaving the agency?" Michelle was almost purring now. "Well, you're the partner on the scene, so it's your call, Liza."

Deep breath. "Then fax me over our standard agreement. We should sign her."

"Sure about that?" Michelle asked. "Because you're the one who'll have to live with this decision. You bring this girl in, she's your client, partner."

That was classic Michelle — direct, hard as nails, and with a sting that any scorpion would envy on the backswing.

Not to mention sharp as a whip. For months, Liza had been working to distance herself from the business of Markson Associates. Taking Jenny Robbins on as a client — launching her career — would represent a new and time-consuming

68

entanglement, complicating all her work to distance herself from that part of her life.

*Oh, what the heck,* Liza thought. *The girl has talent.*

"Let's bag her."

"Are you sure you're up to it? I think you've been getting a little rusty up there in Poontang Bay. You nearly lost me with the first two sentences when you brought this up."

Oh yeah, Michelle was a player. She knew just the right combination of challenge and venom to rope Liza in.

"I think you'll be glad we took Jenny on." Liza was very careful in her choice of pronouns. Michelle would have a definite part to play in getting Jenny established. And frankly, she was necessary. A talent like Jenny's deserved the best representation possible. And that was Michelle — in spades.

"Here's where you can send the contract." Liza reeled off the hotel's fax number. "I'm heading up to Derrick's place early in the morning. She's visiting him."

"You mean he's not waiting around the corner pouring you a nightcap?" Michelle's voice now turned cheerfully mocking. "Old Derrick's still pretty easy on the eyes. And after you spent the winter alone in the cold and fog . . ."

"I never knew *you* to seal a deal that way," Liza shot back. "But then, we don't pry that much into each other's personal lives."

Michelle laughed. "I'll get that fax to you right away. Ysabel is gone, and I've got some airhead from a staffing agency on the front desk. Better I do it myself."

Liza opened her mouth to say something, then shut it. One of her unofficial jobs at the agency had been staff retention — somebody had to step in to fix the effects of Michelle's sometimes caustic remarks. She stopped just in time, recognizing this as another of Michelle's ploys to suck her back in.

"Thanks. I appreciate it," she replied blandly.

Liza was rewarded with another puff of aggravated breath on the other end of the line and a quick cutoff.

She grinned, congratulating herself on having scored a point. Then she checked her watch. Mrs. Halvorsen stayed up to watch the ten o'clock news, and right now the sports would be on — a good time to call.

Liza dialed, and a second later was rewarded with a slightly squeaky voice saying, "Hello?"

If any Hollywood producers needed a prototypical "Little Old Lady," Liza knew exactly where to steer them. "Hi, Mrs. H.," she said. "Liza Kelly here. I just wanted to check in with you — make sure things were okay with Rusty."

"Oh my, yes." Mrs. H.'s voice suddenly turned raspy, and she added a theatrical cough. "I'm afraid, though, the weather was a little raw this evening. I may have caught a chill."

Liza rolled her eyes. Make that a prime hypochondriac "Little Old Lady." The list of ailments that supposedly struck Mrs. Halvorsen would fill a good-sized medical journal. Still, Liza felt a pang of conscience. Had she been asking Mrs. H. to do too much?

Apparently not, judging from what the older woman had to say next. "Rusty is such a good boy, and he does enjoy company. I arranged for someone else to take him for a walk if I feel under the weather."

"I'm hoping to get home before noon," Liza said, "so there should only be a morning walk to worry about." She made a mental note to stop off in Portland and pick up a box of that Scandinavian herb tea Mrs. H. swore by.

"That will be fine. Rusty will be glad to

71

see you." Mrs. H. chuckled. "And I will, too, of course. Have a nice trip, dear. 'The Lord shall preserve thy going out and thy coming in from this time forth, and even for evermore.' That's Psalm 121, verse 8."

The elderly woman's main comfort amid her imaginary illnesses was an ancient family Bible.

*She'd have gotten on with Derrick's dad,* Liza thought, throttling back an urge to respond with an "Amen!"

Instead, she said, "Thanks very much, Mrs. H.," hung up, rose, and stretched to the accompaniment of an enormous yawn. She looked at Will Singleton's puzzles, which she'd unfolded and left beside her bed, intending to start making notes on the solutions. Maybe that was a little optimistic, after today's activities and this evening's wine.

*There's always tomorrow,* Liza told herself. *Maybe I can pick Derrick's brains on the flight. That way I'll have both Will's tournament puzzle and comments by the Hollywood star winner.*

*I like it. And it means I can put off messing with it tonight.*

She'd check at the front desk for Michelle's fax in the morning. Now it was definitely time for bed.

■ ■ ■ ■

The next morning, Liza was up with the dawn again, showering, rooting around in her extremely limited wardrobe, and brewing a cup of coffee in her room's coffeemaker. *Considerably better than what Cal Burke handed me at Ma's,* she thought with a longing look at the little basket of baked goods that had magically appeared outside her door. The croissants looked especially appealing.

No. Derrick had promised her breakfast when she arrived at his place. Regretfully, Liza put the tempting little basket aside uneaten, then turned back on impulse to grab a handful of tiny corn muffins. She wrapped up her stash in a couple of paper napkins and stowed the package in her already loaded carry-on. *That should be enough to make an in-flight snack for both Derrick and me later on,* she thought.

After one last check to make sure she hadn't left anything behind, she headed out the door. She'd already talked to the desk clerk, arranging for a cab to take her up to Derrick's.

Downstairs at the reception desk, Liza picked up the fax from Michelle and checked out. She was riffling through the flimsy sheets of the contract when the cabdriver came into the lobby looking for her. *All present and correct,* she thought as she followed the man out.

The night before, the trip down the mountain roads had been accomplished in pitch darkness. All Liza had gotten from the ride was a sense of numerous twists and turns. Now, seated in the backseat of this cab, she put on her sunglasses to cut the glare of the early-morning sunshine, and let herself stare at the incredible scenery.

It wasn't so obvious at first how scenic the drive was.

The driver's route took them around the outskirts of town, but then they started climbing a narrow road into the mountains. There were indeed plenty of twists and turns as the road wound its way up a series of increasingly rugged slopes.

Soon they'd left the land of manicured lawns behind. Greenery on the cliffsides came from low brush forcing its way between cracks in the rocky walls and trees rooted on ledges above them.

Even in daylight, the driver had to keep both eyes on a road that consisted mostly of hairpin and switchback curves as it kept climbing. Liza, however, was free to enjoy the view. She opened her window, breathing in a slightly rank, piney odor from the trees and bushes. Closing her eyes, she fantasized for a moment that she was back home in Oregon — on a pretty, warm day, she had to admit.

Smiling at her silliness, she opened her eyes, which immediately went very wide. "Stop the car!" she almost screamed.

With a stomp on the brakes, the driver sent them swerving down the road, bringing them to a standstill before he reached the next curve.

Liza was already struggling with the door handle until the driver hit the automatic locks. "You gonna be sick or something?" he asked, anxious about his car's interior.

Liza stumbled out, staring back the way they had come — and upward. Any answer she might have given dried up in her throat as her empty stomach began to roil.

It hadn't been a trick of the shadows. She really had seen a human figure dangling head-down and motionless from the branches of one of the pines. And now she could see the garish pattern on the sweater hanging from the still figure's torso.

It was Derrick Robbins, wearing his not-so-lucky sweater, from the looks of it. Because he was very obviously dead.

# 5

"Hey, lady —" the cabdriver said as he came out of the car. Then he spotted Derrick's body. He froze in his tracks, his jaw sagging open, and almost fell to the pavement. "Holy jumping Judas!"

Liza whipped around. "You've got a radio in your cab, right?"

The driver nodded.

"Then get on it to your base, and have them send the police."

After that, the driver wanted to get out of there. Liza had to use some of the more drastic techniques she'd picked up from Michelle to keep him around. "You're a witness," she told him. "If you drive off, the police could begin to think you're a suspect."

"B-but you're with me," the cabdriver protested. "You chose the destination."

"Precisely. And I'm staying here to talk with them. If you want to make sure what kind of story I tell the police, so will you."

Long minutes passed. Liza spent them with her back determinedly turned to the horrible thing that once had been her friend. Even a quick glance showed that Derrick had hit the mountainside several times before finally getting caught up in the tree. Between the impact wounds and the fact that all the blood had settled in the lower parts of his suspended body, Derrick's handsome face had become a horribly distorted parody of itself. If it weren't for that cheesy sweater —

*Derrick's lucky sweater. The one I'd threatened to throw off the terrace.*

Liza shuddered at the idea. Then another notion hit her. Unless somebody visited after her cab left, she and Jenny were probably among the last people to see Derrick alive.

The arrival of a police cruiser derailed that train of thought. A uniformed officer got out. "We got a report —"

He broke off as he followed the cabdriver's pointing hand, immediately grabbing his car's radio and speaking in a low voice. When he looked at the two of them again, his eyes were suspicious. "You didn't touch . . . ?" The officer broke off that question as he glanced again at the body hanging high above them.

It was patently clear that neither the cabdriver nor Liza was dressed to scale the mountain or climb a tree. If they'd tried it, their clothes would have been in disastrous shape. There was no way that either of them had made the attempt.

"You said in the report of this incident," the cop continued, "that you were going to this gentleman's house?"

Liza nodded. "I had an appointment with him this morning. We were supposed to have breakfast and then head on to his plane for a trip to John Wayne Airport."

The officer had another question for her: Was anyone else at the house? Liza admitted she had no idea. She'd been too rattled to call when she saw her host hanging like a bat from a tree on the mountainside.

She offered to call Derrick's home phone, and the cop took her up on it. When she tried the number, all she got was voice mail.

"Not conclusive," the cop said. "Anybody up in the house could be refusing to answer. Did you pass any other vehicles on the way up here, going either way on the road?"

The cabdriver shook his head. So did Liza.

The questions kept coming, even as backup started to arrive. Between the cab and the cop car, they were blocking the road; nobody could get by.

In the end, the police had the cabbie pull his car to the shoulder of the road. One officer stayed with them while his partner continued on to Derrick's house. From the beady eye the cop aimed at them, Liza didn't have to ask the officer whether she was a suspect. The question in the cop's eyes seemed to be when, not if, to charge her.

While they stood at the roadside, a whole parade of vehicles passed by them — another police cruiser, an ambulance, and what had to be an unmarked police car.

Homicide detectives, Liza figured. Whatever had happened to Derrick, she was willing to bet natural causes had nothing to do with it.

More minutes passed. Then the officer's radio set squawked. Liza couldn't make out what was said, but apparently the cop deciphered it. He turned to the cabdriver. "We're going up. I'll follow you."

Derrick's SUV still stood in the drive in front of the house, just as it had when Liza left the previous night. But it was surrounded by the cavalcade that had passed them while they waited below. There were so many cars parked on the spacious driveway that some of the new vehicles were drawn up on the lawn.

A man in a suit came out of the door, heading straight for Liza. He was tall and powerfully built, with olive skin, dark hair, and features that would have been handsome except for his sullen expression. To Liza, he looked as if his feet hurt — and the expression only intensified as he came closer to her.

"Liza Kelly," the man said, consulting a notebook in his hand. "I'm Detective Vasquez, Santa Barbara Police." He nodded toward the house. "You had a business appointment with Mr. Robbins?"

"More or less. I had worked with Derrick on his last TV series, and he wanted to get my publicity firm to represent his niece." She gave a quick account of how she'd met Derrick, come back with him, seen the screen test, and had dinner. "I was coming up to drop off the representation agreement for Jenny to sign, and then Derrick was going to fly me down to catch a plane to Oregon."

Detective Vasquez nodded impassively, his pen scratching away. "So you were only in the house for the early part of the evening."

"I left at a little around half past nine," Liza told him, "and arrived at the hotel about twenty minutes later."

80

The big man glanced at her over his notebook, his eyes running up and down. "It's a big enough house. Why didn't you stay over?"

Liza shrugged, her face growing a little warm at the detective's insinuation. "I was here on business, so we decided to be businesslike."

Vasquez went back to his notebook. "And Mr. Robbins's niece was with the two of you?"

"Jenny arrived while we were watching her screen test, and we had dinner. The last time I saw her was when she told me that my cab had arrived." Liza paused for a second, steeling herself. "Is she . . . ?"

"She's not on the premises." Vasquez frowned. "Of course, we'll have to search the slope."

Liza winced at that unpleasant assumption.

Vasquez moved on. "Did Ms. Robbins arrive by car?"

"I saw a sporty little compact parked behind Derrick's SUV." Liza frowned, trying to remember any details. "Sorry. It was dark by then; I didn't really notice the make. It was sort of a cream color."

"Obviously, it's gone now." More scratching, then Vasquez snapped the notebook shut. "So, Derrick Robbins was in good spirits, had a pleasant dinner with you and his niece, and expected you this morning for a business meeting."

That pretty much summed things up, but — Liza glanced sharply at Vasquez. Was he suggesting that Derrick had somehow jumped? She took a deep breath, trying to figure out a way to word her question. "Detective? Do you have any theory on how Derrick . . . fell?"

"That's what we're trying to figure out." Vasquez's large hand closed on Liza's upper arm — a surprisingly gentle grasp. "I'd like you to look at some things inside the house."

"Anything I can do to help," she said as the detective conducted her to the door. Vasquez had her retrace her steps through the house, to the bathroom, the home theater, the kitchen, and then out onto the terrace. She noticed immediately that one wrought-iron chair — Derrick's seat during supper — was now overturned, its upholstered padding ripped loose. Nearby, one of the planters atop the low wall lay overturned on the flagstones, several flowering shrubs pulled out by the roots. It looked as if some sort of struggle had taken place.

*They're not trying to figure out how Derrick fell,* she thought. *They suspect he was pushed.* And judging from the way Detective Vasquez was looking at her, she apparently topped his candidate list as the pusher.

Another man in a suit turned away from where technicians were photographing the torn shrubbery. He was short and rotund, with a jolly face, until you looked closely at his eyes — a little too cold and watchful. Cop's eyes. "Liza Kelly, my partner, Detective Howard."

Howard gave her a broad smile, as if he were delighted to meet her.

*I guess this is the good cop,* Liza thought.

"I don't suppose you can tell us anything about this?" Howard asked jovially.

Liza shook her head. "It was all in order when we cleaned the dinner dishes away." She stepped toward the overturned chair. Both Vasquez and Howard moved to block her, so she stopped and pointed. Beside the disarranged padding lay a broken glass, short, squat, and cylindrical.

"That highball glass wasn't out here. We only drank wine."

Vasquez's notebook came out again.

"There were no disagreements at dinner — no arguments?" Howard asked.

Liza shook her head. "I was mainly getting to know Jenny." She smiled at the memory of dinner. "Derrick always has —

*had* — a good line of funny conversation. He could toss off some outrageous statements, but you couldn't call them arguments."

She suddenly remembered his claim about the coded sudoku messages. Was that worth mentioning?

The two detectives must have noticed her hesitation but said nothing.

"Did you go anywhere else from here?" Howard asked.

Liza brought them to Derrick's study. The door stood open, and she stood open-mouthed at the entrance to the room. The calm order she had noticed the night before had vanished. Where the built-in shelves had boasted carefully arranged ranks of books, now it looked as if Derrick were running a rummage sale.

"This isn't right," she said. "Derrick grouped his books by subject. He was into puzzles and codes." She pointed. "This whole shelf held books about sudoku. Now it's all messed up. There are books about acrostics and cryptography mixed in. Some of them are upside down, and look — that one's stuffed in backward."

Howard glanced at his partner. "Looks like a job for the fingerprint boys." He turned back to Liza. "Was there anything valuable in here?"

"I didn't look at all the titles." Liza was still in shock, her eyes roving around. "Two things seem to be missing — a newspaper and an old Gideon Bible." She carefully scanned the bookshelves but didn't see a trace of the worn leatherette cover.

"That doesn't —" Howard began, but Liza cut him off.

"He was trying to decode something," she said slowly, trying to dredge up memories of their uncomfortable conversation in this very room — a conversation where she hadn't really paid much attention. Haltingly, Liza tried to explain Derrick's concern over the *Seattle Prospect*'s sudoku puzzles — how they seemed to contain biblical references that turned into unpleasant real-life events. "He mentioned something about people grumbling and being burned — that it wasn't the Lord's fire."

Liza stumbled to a halt. Like Derrick, she'd lost her audience. Detective Howard looked attentive, but his eyes were hooded. Detective Vasquez, who didn't have to worry about being the good cop, simply stared at her as if she were out of her mind.

"Do you know if Robbins had any history of mental problems?" Mr. Sensitivity now looked as if she'd stepped on his aching feet.

Howard put it a bit more tactfully. "I seem to remember that Mr. Robbins tended to play troubled or . . . eccentric characters."

"He was playing roles," Liza replied. "It's called acting. Derrick was one of the most dependable people on the set — he wasn't a nut case. He was a very intelligent man."

"He was an actor who hadn't worked in . . . what? The last year? Year and a half?" Howard asked.

Vasquez didn't even bother to argue. "We'll get the crime-scene people in here," he grunted. "And I suppose we should bring you down to the station and get a statement."

His tone suggested how credible he thought that statement would be.

Liza decided to save her breath rather than argue with the big man. Silently, she sat in the rear of the unmarked car — *Where the prisoners go,* she thought — while Vasquez drove downtown. Detective Howard stayed at the scene of what Liza now firmly believed was a crime.

The police station was a two-story building, in the Spanish colonial architectural style seemingly required for Southern California. Liza barely got an impression of gleaming white walls and reddish orange roof tiles as Detective Vasquez brought her in. Liza took off her sunglasses when she heard a voice call out her name.

She focused on a short, bald man who looked like a living, breathing Elmer Fudd. But that pudgy face was known to everyone who watched Court TV — or even the national news. Alvin Hunzinger might not look very Hollywood, but he'd earned the nickname of "lawyer to the stars" in a series of high-profile cases.

Right now, he cast a bemused glance at Liza — Elmer at his most befuddled. Most of his practice involved movie stars as perpetrators, not victims. "Michelle Markson sent me up here," he said in a voice as silky as Elmer's was silly.

Liza shook her head, hiding a smile. Trust Michelle to get in ahead of everyone. Her intelligence sources must rival the CIA's.

Alvin turned to Detective Vasquez, extending a hand. "I'm —"

"I know who you are," Vasquez snarled, definitely not amused. In fact, if she'd been judging by the look on his face, Liza would have thought that Alvin had just driven spikes through both of the cop's long-suffering feet.

■ ■ ■ ■

# PART TWO:
## SOLVING

■ ■ ■ ■

When you come down to it, sudoku is always about the same thing — filling in eighty-one spaces where between twenty-odd to forty-odd spaces have been filled in already. The question becomes, what techniques do you use to fill up the empties?

"Easy" sudoku need only a few techniques. With a simple scan of the rows and columns, you can see the only numbers that will fit in certain spaces. A more detailed search fills more spaces, and the logical interaction of filled spaces in rows, columns, and squares forces solutions. The harder the puzzle, however, the farther you have to stretch this logic, until, at the greatest levels of difficulty, it may be hard to distinguish between a logical technique and inspired guesswork.

— Excerpt from *Sudo-cues* by Liza K

# 6

Hours later, Liza had to wonder if she'd made the right decision. She'd accepted Alvin Hunzinger's services, infuriating Detective Vasquez. But she'd also annoyed Alvin by stubbornly staying while Vasquez and several other detectives questioned her over her statement. They spent considerable time pecking away at any inconsistencies while Liza labored to tell them as much about the previous evening as she could remember.

Alvin's pudgy face took on a pained expression as Liza kept trying to bring up Derrick's story about secret messages in the Seattle paper. Vasquez and his colleagues kept cutting her off, asking questions about her relationship with Derrick, or Jenny, or with anyone who might bear a grudge against him.

At last, the lawyer rose and said, "Excuse me, Detectives, but I have some business to take care of. I'm advising my client to say nothing in my absence." He turned a very un–Elmer Fudd stare at Liza. "Understand?"

Liza silently nodded yes.

As soon as Alvin was out of the interrogation room, Vasquez jumped out of his chair. "Okay, so maybe you don't want to talk, but you're sure as hell going to listen." His normally sullen features looked more like a thundercloud about to blast the ground. "Innocent people usually don't lawyer up when they come down to give a statement." He thrust his face closer to Liza's. "And they usually don't have a hot-dog lawyer waiting for them when they arrive at the station."

After that, the interrogators ignored Liza, even to the extent of arguing over the conduct of the case. "We're wasting time here," the female cop who'd taken Detective Howard's place insisted. "There are other leads —"

"Not till Howard finishes the search down the slope," Vasquez replied.

Liza's empty stomach lurched at the thought of Jenny Robbins's broken body lying somewhere far below the terrace.

At last Alvin returned, accompanied by a man Liza found vaguely familiar. "This is

Josh Marsh, a driver for SB Taxi," he announced, then asked the man, "Is your passenger from last night in here?"

Liza hadn't remembered the driver's face, but the nasal voice he used in his response was instantly recognizable. "Sure. It's the lady over there." He pointed at Liza.

"Do you recall when you picked her up?"

Marsh nodded. "I checked my logbook. It was 9:37, at a fancy place up in the mountains."

"Was the lady alone when you picked her up?" Alvin asked.

"Nah. A girl opened the door, and a guy came out to wave good-bye while this lady got in my car."

"Did you recognize the man?"

"Yeah, he was that hot-shi—" The driver glanced over at Liza. "That hotshot actor who used to be on the spy show. My wife is crazy about him. She was all over me this morning when I mentioned it, because I didn't try to get his autograph."

The only thing missing from Alvin's self-satisfied smile was the Elmer Fudd "huh-huh-huh" laugh. "I believe this establishes that everyone in the house was alive and well when my client departed," he said. "If you have nothing further . . . ?"

"Ms. Kelly, you can go," Vasquez ground

out through gritted teeth.

"But what about — ?" Liza began.

Vasquez cut her off. "Go," he said.

The female detective was more diplomatic. "We have your information and can get in touch with you if needed."

"My client will make herself available," Alvin promised.

"Right. Great." Vasquez made shooing motions. Liza might make herself available, but he obviously wasn't going to be sitting by the phone.

Alvin hadn't just spent his time digging up a witness. He'd also gotten Liza a seat on a plane to Portland. "Pretty confident, weren't you?" she said in his car around a mouthful of corn muffin.

"Reasonably assured." The lawyer to the stars looked pained at the sight of crumbs on his upholstery, then turned apprehensive eyes to Liza. "You'll tell Michelle I did my best for you?"

"Of course, Alvin," she replied, a little mystified. "I promise."

"Good, good." He reached into the inside pocket of his jacket and handed Liza her ticket. "I'm afraid you missed the direct flight. This is the next one out."

A moment later, Liza realized she'd been the victim of a little legal maneuver. Alvin had extracted her promise before she looked at the tickets.

"Santa Barbara to Portland — by way of Phoenix, Arizona? You didn't accidentally book me for Portland, Maine, did you?"

Unfortunately, Alvin hadn't. So a journey that should have taken a couple of hours wound up costing Liza six hours and change — and that didn't count the drive from Portland southwest to Maiden's Bay.

Liza had tried to fill some of her plane time making notes on Will's puzzle for her column. Remembering how she'd planned to do this with Derrick left her too heartsick — and tired — to go on. After barely a page of notes, she knocked off with a feeling of frustration. Some of the most basic techniques wouldn't even work with this puzzle. *Wait a minute. I've got the nincompoop's version — ahem, the entry round version — too,* she thought ruefully.

It had been full dark for almost an hour by the time Liza pulled up in front of her house. She'd gotten some sleep on the various planes, but came out of it disoriented, dehydrated, and just plain frazzled.

"Thank God I made it," Liza muttered as she slipped her key into the front door lock. It was pulled out of her hand as the door suddenly swung open, revealing a large male figure silhouetted against the living-room lamplight.

Flinging her bag aside, Liza jumped back, bringing her arms up. What do to? Scream or run?

"Liza?" the figure said, stepping aside to pick up her carry-on. "Are you okay?"

Now standing in the light from the door, the menacing form became part of the normal world — or more precisely, ancient history. Kevin Shepard was the guy Liza had gone out with in high school.

"What are *you* doing here?" she asked in astonishment.

"Taking care of the dog," Kevin replied, a little shamefacedly. "I got a call from Mrs. Halvorsen, sounding as if she was at death's door. As far as I could make out, her last wish was that I should take care of her neighbor's dog. It's only when I got here that I remembered . . . um, realized . . ."

Liza took the bag from his hand, shaking her head. *Sheesh! Everybody is taking advantage of me today!*

Besides collecting illnesses and reading scripture, Mrs. H. had one other pastime — matchmaking. Maybe it tied in with that "be fruitful and multiply" line from the Bible.

Confronted with a much longer than

expected trip, Liza had phoned her neighbor from the Santa Barbara airport. Mrs. H. had assured her that someone would be over to feed and walk Rusty. *I just didn't expect my prom date,* Liza thought crossly.

She had to admit, though, that Kevin was looking well. For almost fifteen years, she'd only caught quick, distant glimpses of him during whirlwind visits back home.

*Don't say something stupid,* Liza warned herself as she opened her mouth.

She was saved as a furry, reddish thunderbolt came streaking out the door, a wagging tail at one end and a rattling leash dragging from the other.

"We were going for a walk," Kevin explained.

Rusty gave a low *woof* of welcome when he saw Liza. But he brought the leash over to Kevin, who apparently had become his new best friend. That was a surprise. Rusty loved being with kids, but he wasn't fond of larger men — probably the result of some unpleasant incident from his wandering days.

Not, Liza thought, that Kevin was *too* big. He'd been tall and rangy, the school's second-string football star, when they went out together. *He's filled out nicely in the years since,* she thought, looking on appreciatively as Kevin bent to put the leash on Rusty.

The reel almost flew out of Kevin's hand when Rusty ran to the end of its full tether. Obviously, he'd been bursting to get out. Kevin laughed as Rusty trotted around, snuffling for a place to irrigate. "I've hooked full-grown salmon that didn't make the reel spin like that."

"Are you still in the guide business?" Liza asked. That had been Kevin's ambition back when — a business that didn't require college. He'd gone into the army while Liza went off to school, serving in Desert Storm — aka Iraq, Chapter One. Coming home, he'd tried to put his Special Forces training to use in the mountains and rivers. Liza had heard he'd also picked up a wife along the way.

"Not exactly," Kevin replied. "I ended up reevaluating my life a couple years ago — after the divorce." His voice got a bit flat. "Took a couple of courses, and I'm managing a place down in Killamook."

"The preservation capital of the Northwest coast?" Liza said in shock. "I never thought you'd let a town council tell you what color you could paint your shutters."

Kevin grinned. "The Killamook Inn is outside the town proper. We look properly rustic, and we kick in too much tax money for them to complain much."

Liza nodded. She'd heard of the Killamook Inn, a resort sufficiently ritzy to consider using for some of Markson Associates' clients.

Looking off into the darkness, Kevin added, "Of course, I always hear about your exciting life down in Hollywood. I understand you got married."

"And I moved back here to think that over," Liza told him.

He glanced over at her, but before he could say anything, a commotion broke out in the shrubbery where Rusty was nosing around. The dog began growling and barking.

"Is anybody out there?" Liza called, suddenly thinking of Hank Lovelorn — *Lonebaugh,* she quickly corrected herself. He had disappeared from the hotel after his humiliation at the tournament. In fact, she still had his handheld sudoku solver, having promised Will that she'd return it to Hank.

Maybe he'd come over to retrieve his doodad and had run out of nerve. Maybe he was debating whether his ego could take an embarrassing meeting right now. Maybe he'd heard about Derrick on the news and come over to talk.

*Or maybe,* an unpleasant voice in the back

of her head suggested, *he's out there in the underbrush staring at you like a common, garden-variety stalker.*

As Rusty kept barking, a figure emerged from the bushes — a large, shambling figure, built much more solidly than Hank. Liza made a little sound of surprise as she recognized Calvin Burke.

"Hey, Cal," Kevin said, reeling in the leash as he and Liza walked out to stand by Rusty.

Liza glanced between the two men. Fifteen years ago, they'd often sat in Ma's Café, enjoying a soda on the house. Cal was the big man on campus, fast as well as big, leading the football team to three regional championships. Scouts from colleges all over the West Coast had flocked to town, and Cal had gone off on a football scholarship, a stepping-stone to the NFL.

That was before he blew out a knee. Under NCAA rules, he wasn't supposed to lose his scholarship but the athletic department could reduce his aid. And when tuition went up . . . well, that was the end of Cal and college. When Liza came back to her hometown, she found the football hero she'd remembered had become a not-so-proficient handyman, smelling of beer during the day and often falling-down drunk by the end of the night.

This was a bit early, though.

"Ma's cat got out," Calvin said, brushing himself off. "I thought I heard her in there." He looked down and started brushing ineffectually at his pants leg with a tattered piece of tissue.

"Oh God! Rusty didn't —" Liza rushed up with a bigger wad of tissue. Calvin winced as she pressed it against the damp spot. "The bad leg," he muttered. "Y'know how people always say you get used to things with age? They fricking lie."

He gave Kevin the ghost of a smile. "Good to see you again, guy. You and Liza — just like old times, huh?" Wrapping a bit of threadbare dignity around himself, he limped off — somewhat undercutting the effect by pinching at his trouser leg and shaking it.

Rusty had calmed down after Liza and Kevin had joined him. Now he shook himself, making his dog tags rattle, and led them off again.

Maiden's Bay was not a big town for nightlife. People put in a day's work and usually spent a couple hours in front of the tube before turning in to get ready for the next day. Definitely Dullsville in the eyes of people from — or aspiring to — a happening town like L.A. Or was it? As she walked with Kevin and Rusty down the quiet streets, Liza found herself enjoying an expatriate's appreciation of her old hometown — the weathered cedar houses, many of them surrounded by beds of azaleas so thick, the silvery wood structures seemed to be floating on clouds.

"Memorial Day is coming up," Kevin mentioned as they passed the little traffic circle around the monument to the World War II dead. "I have to order a wreath."

"I thought the parade was over in Killamook," Liza said.

"Yeah, they're turning the place into a small-town theme park to pack the tourists in," Kevin grumbled. "Every marching band and fire department in the county is expected to turn out. But I get together with a couple of local buddies from the VFW and do a quiet ceremony here." He glanced at her. "After all, this is still my hometown."

The business district was already shuttered as they passed through, but Rusty led them across the highway and into the industrial area by the shore, determined to investigate the various interesting smells coming from the harbor. Kevin allowed him to unreel the leash onto the docks from the landward end of the block-long boardwalk.

"I hate seeing Cal like that," Kevin said

quietly. "I guess you missed most of it, being away in school and then going off to Japan."

"When Dad died, Mom wanted me to go over there and see her side of the family," Liza said. "It was kind of a shock when Mom passed away and I came back up here. You know, everyone calls him Calvin now."

"I know," Kevin said. "I was away in the army when it all happened. Maybe if I had been here, Cal wouldn't have had such a crash landing."

He turned guilty eyes to Liza. "It's one of the reasons I don't come in to Maiden's Bay much anymore." He paused. "That, and hearing that you'd come back to town. It's not all that far to Killamook, and the town council hasn't yet legislated the small-town grapevine out of existence."

"It is very traditional," Liza murmured. Rusty had finished sniffing around and began leading them home.

"Anyway, when Mrs. H. called, I drove over," Kevin said. "She was a friend of my grandmother's, you know. I just never thought — and now, I guess I'm glad it happened. I don't think I'd have had the nerve to come poking around otherwise."

Soon, they were back in front of the house. Liza got out her keys again, and

103

Kevin handed her the leash. She was just about to invite him in for coffee when the phone inside began to ring.

Liza handed back the leash. "Would you mind holding on for a minute?" After being buzzed twice by Michelle on the trip home — and not accepting the calls — Liza had finally turned off her cell phone. *Guess now I'll have to face the music,* she thought.

Hurrying inside, she crossed the little living room to the kitchen, where she caught the phone on the fifth ring. "Hello?"

The voice on the other end wasn't female, though. "Are you all right? It's Michael."

Liza stared at the phone, caught by surprise. At her hesitation, the voice went from worried to acid. "You remember — the guy you married?"

# 7

"Could you hold on for a moment?" Liza said to Michael. Putting down the phone, she went to the door and took Rusty's leash. "I've got to take this," she whispered to Kevin.

His eyes showed a momentary flash of — what? Disappointment?

*You wish,* Liza told herself.

Then, with a wry grin, Kevin nodded. "Sure. See you." He walked off without even trying for a kiss.

Going back to the phone, Liza explained, "I was out walking the dog."

Michael made a noncommittal noise. During their years together, his allergies had kept them from having any pets.

Liza imagined him in his usual pose, sprawled on the couch in their living room, holding the cordless phone to his ear with one hand while brushing back an errant dark curl with the other. Books were the major décor item in their small house (only movie stars, producers, and embezzling energy magnates could afford large houses in Southern California).

Of course, there'd be gaps on the bookshelves now, since Liza had taken most of her books up to Oregon. Except for sudoku volumes, most of her library occupied boxes in the spare room.

They'd had a symbiotic relationship — she was a reader, and Michael was a writer. Mostly, he made a living creating novels for book packagers under various pseudonyms and doing script doctoring for movie producers who specialized in direct-to-video product. Of course, he had several screenplays of his own that he hoped to sell. Up to the point where they'd separated, however, the closest he'd come to doing that was a development stint on a kiddie show.

*Rip-Roaring Rocket Rovers* involved cobbling together action sequences from Japanese ninja sci-fi movies (where the Asian stuntmen conveniently wore jet packs and full space suits with helmets) with bridging scenes featuring Caucasian actors. Then the series went into production up in Vancouver, where only Canadian writers could work. The gig had gotten Michael script-doctoring assignments in Poverty Row, but that had made the situation worse. As Liza's publicity career had advanced, Michael's work seemed to push him further into the background.

His basically quiet nature hadn't helped, either. Oh, he'd gotten a bit more waspish, but most of the time he simply seemed to lose himself in the sudoku he usually used for entertainment during dry spells. Then he'd left.

That brought a lot of things to a head. And since the tenant in Mom's old house in Maiden's Bay had just left, it seemed more reasonable for Liza to come up here to take a shot at sorting her life out while Michael came back to their Westwood house from the motel where he'd been staying.

Well, Michael was talking now. "I've been trying to get hold of you for hours," he complained. "If I hadn't recognized your voice on the tape, I'd have thought you changed the number on me. As if I didn't have enough on my plate, fielding more wacko phone calls than I can count."

"I wound up on a very long flight back from Santa Barbara and didn't want to spend it on the phone," Liza said.

"We were on the ten o'clock news — they ran a clip of us on the red carpet for the Oscars three years ago." A trace of bitterness welled up in Michael's voice again. "Apparently, that reminded a bunch of people about me. All of a sudden, newspeople began calling in. Some were legit — the networks and cable news — and then there were the other ones. All the celebrity TV shows wanted me on camera — *Entertainment Evening, Showbiz News, Hollywood Special Edition.* All the bloodsuckers you made nice to over the years."

What could Liza say to that? Dealing with those bloodsuckers had indeed been part of her business. She'd never kidded herself that these were her friends. "Yeah, well," she finally told Michael, "I imagine that would raise your profile."

"Right," he snorted. "Just what I'd want. A couple of calls from the print tabloid people showed me exactly what I could expect if they got me on camera. The tabloid guys were connecting you and Derrick Robbins in all kinds of interesting ways." He waited for a long moment for her to respond to that.

Liza didn't.

"The smart money figures you did it," Michael went on, "but Michelle Markson and Alvin Hunzinger will get you off. They tell me old Alvin has been batting .667 so far this year. He got a dismissal for whatshisname — that comedian who drowned his wife, and the judge just talked sternly to Roughhouse Kearns." Rufus Kearns was a fading action star who'd gotten drunk and fired a shotgun at his yardman. That was a case that had made the national media as well as the supermarket newspapers.

"I can't believe Alvin had the nerve to play the race card in that case — saying that Roughhouse saw a dark face and acted instinctively to protect his house."

Liza grimaced at the hypocrisy. Most of upper-crust L.A. had people with dark faces tending their gardens, their pools, their cars, and carrying trays at their parties.

"And your producer pal whose pregnant girlfriend went off Mulholland Drive in his Maserati only got nailed in the civil suit," Michael concluded, his voice sounding a little slurred on the last words.

*Has he been drinking?* Liza wondered but didn't want to ask.

"Don't worry, I didn't have anything to say to those news creeps. Figured that's the way you would want it, even if you weren't around to talk to."

Michael's voice got a little more blurry — some complaint that Liza couldn't catch. "What I did was refer them to Michelle. She probably ground them up."

"So what is the dumb money saying?" Liza asked, hoping to keep things light.

Unfortunately, Michael took her literally. "I'd say they're evenly split between you and Jenny Robbins. Some people just aren't buying the whole 'niece' thing. The fact that she's disappeared doesn't look good."

He laughed a little too loudly, a sure sign he had been drinking. "I'll tell you the theory the guy from the *National Yell* ran past me. He's going with the idea of a three-way relationship between you, Derrick, and Jenny. Asked me to comment on the suggestion that you killed Jenny out of jealousy, and then turned against Derrick. He expects that Jenny will turn up farther down the mountain because she's lighter — you could throw her farther out from the terrace. It's just bad luck that Derrick got caught in a tree."

His boozy lightheartedness suddenly evaporated. "I hung up on the bastard."

Michael took a long, steadying breath. "What happened down there, Liza?"

She gave him the whole story — meeting Derrick at a sudoku tournament, going up to Santa Barbara to see the screen test, her dinner with Derrick and Jenny. But when she started to tell Michael about Derrick's suspicions of secret messages in the Seattle paper's sudoku, he snorted in disbelief.

"Oh, come on, Liza. I guess it's just as well this conspiracy theory stuff didn't get out. It would make Derrick look like a Looney Toon." He paused for a second. "And you, too."

"Thanks a lot," Liza responded. She paused. "You sound more sober now."

"Well, I guess what you had to say shocked me sober," Michael told her.

But Liza wasn't about to laugh this off. "Michael, that's what Derrick told me."

"I don't doubt it. What surprises me is that you sound like you believe it. Hey, this stuff makes the lamebrained plot twists in the scripts I doctor sound calm and rational. You said yourself this guy has had a lot of time on his hands since his series went off. All of a sudden, he's finding Bible messages in sudoku? Maybe he found God talking to him in his crossword, so he jumped."

"That's not funny, Michael," Liza choked out. "You weren't out on that terrace. There was a fight — and Derrick was thrown off."

"Okay, okay," Michael said. "But it could have been a home invasion — something with no connection to anything else."

"Don't you think that's stretching a coincidence?" Liza objected.

"But having him killed over a conspiracy

theory isn't." Michael laughed. "You'd think people would have finally gotten over *The Da Vinci Code* by now."

Liza stood in silence with the phone to her ear. She didn't like the way this whole discussion had gone, but was it worth an argument to bring it up again?

"Look, I just got in touch to make sure you were all right and see if there's any help you need." That surly tone crept back into Michael's voice. "Although I suppose with Michelle and the lawyer from hell on your side, I probably wasted a call."

"Michael —" Liza began, then sighed. "I'll just say thanks, all right?"

She hung up, shaking her head. Talking to Kevin tonight, after having him appear out of nowhere, it was as if he'd never gone out of her life. Michael's call, after a couple months of separation, left her wondering if she'd ever known him at all.

"One thing is certain," she told Rusty. "If I'm going to make any sense out of what happened, it looks like I'll have to solve the damn thing myself."

## 8

Liza's lips quirked in a smile as Rusty cocked his head and looked up at her. "Right," she said. "It sounds good, but how do I make it happen?"

Obviously, she'd need help, somebody who knew as much about codes as Liza knew about sudoku. Liza made a little pumping motion with her fist as she realized she might know just the person — Uncle Jim!

Like Liza's mother, Uncle Jim Watanabe was Japanese American, born and raised in the States. Unlike Mom, however, Uncle Jim had lived in Japan for most of the last thirty years, working in the American embassy. Liza hadn't really thought about it, even during the months she'd spent in Japan after college. But would the State Department really give someone a posting that lasted for decades?

Uncle Jim had been the one to introduce

Liza to sudoku. The number puzzles had been a lifesaver for a girl with a very shaky grasp of the Japanese language and an even shakier knowledge of the country's underlying culture. But numbers and logic are universal, and Liza's knack for sudoku — she even created puzzles — had helped to build a bridge to her Japanese relatives.

Nowadays, reading about the finally declassified Cold War exploits of U.S. Navy submarines sneaking through the Sea of Japan to tap underwater Soviet cables for information, Liza wondered more about what exactly her uncle had gotten up to in the embassy. He'd always been extremely closedmouthed about his work . . .

Whatever it was, it definitely wasn't a nine-to-five job. Liza got on her computer, intending to go online and leave an e-mail for her relative. Even though it had to be 4 a.m. over there, Uncle Jim responded with an instant message.

What are you doing up at such an ungodly hour? Liza typed.

Working late. A quick answer, but as usual with Uncle Jim, it didn't tell much.

I guess the news hasn't hit over there yet, she began, giving a brief version of Derrick's death — and his suspicions. I tried to tell the police, she finished. They pretty much blew me off.

The IM box on her screen remained empty for long moments, then came the sign that Uncle Jim was typing. Codes in sudoku? Possible.

After another pause, more words appeared. Could be a book code.

What's that? Liza immediately typed back.

It would look like a string of numbers. Uncle Jim replied. But it actually breaks down to a series of directions to find a word in a line, the line on the page, and the page number where you're supposed to look.

A string of numbers — that could describe any row or column in a sudoku puzzle. But the rules of the game meant that no numbers could be repeated. The keyboard rattled under Liza's fingers as she raised this objection.

Given a fat enough book, you could find enough words to send messages and still fall under sudoku constraints. Uncle Jim responded.

Derrick mentioned the Bible. Liza typed.

Depending on the edition, could run 1,000–1,500 pages or more. Uncle Jim's reply quickly appeared on the screen. Fat enough, IMO.

Liza couldn't help her curiosity. How do you know so much about codes?

Like your friend, I read a lot of books. Came

the bland but uninformative response. She could just imagine Uncle Jim saying that, a polite smile on an otherwise poker face.

Any puzzle will give you 18 number strings, 36 if you read them backward. Her uncle warned. None will make sense unless you have the correct edition.

Got that, I think. Liza replied. Ill chek out an let you know. Her typing always went downhill when she was excited, and right now she wanted to start checking on Gideon Bibles. Uncle Jim wished her good luck, she thanked him, and then Liza began Googling for Gideon Bibles.

When she got to the Gideons' website, however, she hit a major snag. Instead of having one Bible for nationwide distribution, regional groups bought different publishers' editions of the Good Book for delivery to local hotels, motels, and prisons.

Liza frowned, trying to dredge up memories of Derrick talking about his past. His family had come from somewhere in Indiana to settle in St. Louis, she recalled. And his dad's sales territory was in the rural South — she remembered some funny stories about that.

Derrick's father must have gotten that Gideon Bible somewhere down South a good thirty years ago. So how could a guy on the West Coast wind up with the exact same Bible to send secret messages in a book code?

*Another bright idea bites the dust,* she thought. Then she brightened as she thought of another way to attack the problem.

Liza turned to her phone, resolutely ignoring the balefully blinking red light on her answering machine. *Those I can deal with tomorrow,* she thought. Most of them were probably people she didn't even want to deal with, anyway. Right now, there were only two people she wanted to speak with, and she began dialing one of them.

The phone on the other end ran through enough rings that Liza began to worry that the answering machine would pick up. Instead, it was answered by a human voice, if a rather groggy one.

"Did I wake you up, Will?" she asked with a guilty glance at the clock.

"No, no, I was just resting my eyes," Will Singleton lied politely. "What's up, Liza? Something to do with the article you want to do on my puzzles? When you came up to ask for those copies, I thought you were going to curse me out for luring you into the same hotel with Derrick Robbins. But that turned out pretty well, except for the young fellow leaving his little computer. Did you get in touch with him?"

He paused, suddenly sounding even more tired. "Or is this about what happened to Derrick? I did hear about it on the news, but I seem to be having a hard time wrapping my mind around it."

"I'm sorry," Liza said awkwardly. Will and Derrick must have been friends, even if she hadn't known about it. "Between talking with the police and getting back home, it seems like almost a week ago," she admitted. "But the news must have been quite a shock."

She paused. "I have an odd question for you, I'm afraid. Do you know who does the sudoku for the *Seattle Prospect*?"

"Funny you should ask that," Will said. "Poor Derrick was talking with me about the same thing during the tournament. I'm afraid I got dragged off in the middle of the conversation, but I'll tell you exactly what I told him — I don't know."

He sounded almost defensive at Liza's silent response. "Well, you can't expect me to know *everything* there is to know about sudoku." He chuckled. "I'll tell you one thing, though. Whoever it is, he and/or she did a better job of hiding their interest in sudoku than you did."

"So what does the *Prospect* say? 'Puzzles

by Mystery Person'? "

"They'd probably jump at that idea," Will replied. "The *Prospect* represents an American toehold by yet another Australian media magnate, a character named Ward Dexter. He followed the Murdoch method, buying a failing American paper. Then he filled the staff with a bunch of smart-ass Aussies and the pages with celebrity gossip and features. Only he decided to conquer America from the Left Coast, and he hasn't bought a Hollywood studio yet. I don't think he's quite in that league."

He was silent for a moment, checking the monumental database he called a memory. "Whoever does the puzzles must be a good conservative, though — Dexter would insist on that. Although, oddly enough, I know this person disregards one puzzle-making tradition. You know how crosswords start off with easy puzzles early in the week, working up to a Saturday or Sunday stumper?"

"Sure," Liza replied. "I do the same with my sudoku for the *Oregon Daily*."

"Well, this person, whoever it may be, doesn't do that," Will said. "Sometimes, you'll find an absolute killer in Monday's paper and one that novices could do in their sleep on Sunday."

119

Liza frowned into the phone, digesting this information. She heard Will clear his throat over the phone line.

"All right. I've done my best to satisfy your curiosity. Now I hope you'll satisfy mine. What's going on, Liza? The more I think about this, the less I like the idea of you asking the same questions Derrick did before . . . whatever happened to him."

"If I tell you, you have to promise you won't tell a soul," Liza said.

"You know I can keep a secret." Will sounded hurt. "Look at how long I've known about you and sudoku."

*Yeah — and you only blabbed it to Derrick — I hope,* Liza thought. Still, if she hoped to get anywhere with her investigation, she'd probably need Will's knowledge and contacts. Taking a deep breath, she gave Will the short version of Derrick's suspicions.

The line remained silent for a long moment after she finished. "Now I wish I'd had the time for a real talk with Derrick," Will said quietly. "Although, at the time, I would have had a dark suspicion that he was merely setting me up for some sort of gag."

Now it was Liza's turn to go silent. Derrick was a really good actor when he wanted to be. He'd taken some pretty hokey stuff scripted into *Spycraft* and made it work. However, when he wasn't being serious, Derrick had a dreadful reputation for pranks. Suppose Michael was right, and an unconnected crime had coincidentally ruined Derrick's "Oooh! Scary, boys and girls!" setup for some silly joke?

"I brushed it off myself." She shook her head. "But looking back, I think Derrick was serious — dead serious. And there's something else. After I found Derrick, the police had me in his study. The room looked as if a pack of monkeys had gone through it. Everything was just shoved back on the shelves."

"That definitely wasn't Derrick. His puzzle library had been a special project. He asked for my opinion on some of the acquisitions, personally bought each book, designed the bookshelves, and arranged them all himself." Will sounded as if he'd come to a decision of some sort. "If you're going to try decrypting any puzzles, you're going to need more computing ability than any home model can give you. Hold on a moment —"

The phone went down with a muted thump — probably on a pile of papers, Liza thought, given Will's work methods.

"Got it," he said, getting back on the line.

"This is the number for Max Frisch. He's a professor at Coastal University and quite the sudoku fiend. I bet he'll be quite impressed to discover that Liza K is a neighbor of sorts — and he has access to the university's computer system. The big mainframes, if you know what I mean."

Liza thanked Will, cautioned him to silence one more time, wished him good night, and hung up.

One more call. Liza dialed Michelle's private cell number with some trepidation. After two rings, she got a connection.

"Finally." Michelle had obviously checked the incoming number before answering. The background noise — chattering voices, clinking glasses — muted as Liza's partner walked away from the party. Sometimes it seemed as if Michelle attended a party every evening — an opening, an awards event, a client's anniversary of some sort.

"I won't insult you by going over the basics, like not talking to reporters," Michelle said.

Liza looked at her blinking answering machine. "I've only been on the phone with two people — and neither of them has any connection with the media."

"Just refer everyone to the agency. We've

been handling everything since this morning."

"And what are you telling everyone without me around to say anything?" Liza couldn't help asking.

"The barest of facts, that you were seeing Derrick Robbins on business and had discovered his body while bringing him a contract. No speculations about mysterious messages or murderous nieces."

"How — ?" Even as the question was forced out of her, Liza had to shake her head in reluctant admiration at the way her partner kept abreast of everything.

"Unlike some people, Alvin called very promptly to discuss the situation," Michelle replied. "That will do for the present. For everything else . . . my office — tomorrow, two o'clock."

She probably began ringing off halfway through Liza's assent.

Liza turned back to her computer. As expected, there was a very recent e-mail from Markson Associates with the confirmation codes for round-trip flights between PDX and LAX. *Not* too *self-assured, our Michelle,* she thought wryly.

The flight from Portland left around 11:00 a.m. At least she wouldn't have to get up with the sun again. The return trip would land her around 6:00 p.m.

That meant she'd be losing most of a day's work tomorrow. *Better check in at work. I've got a couple of backup columns I can plug in, and I think I'm still a week ahead on puzzles. Maybe I can work up a column out of Will's puzzle while I'm traveling back and forth from La-la Land . . .*

A few clicks of the mouse, and Liza had the login screen for the *Oregon Daily*'s computer network. She typed in the password for her account, and then leaned back in her chair, frowning in surprise.

According to her computer, her account was already being accessed!

# 9

Liza had enough time for a brief run the next morning — something Rusty always liked. He apparently saw it as a race and did his best to take and maintain the lead. By the time they returned home, his tongue was lolling, and Liza was panting. *Too much time on my butt in airplanes,* she thought darkly. *And I'll be doing it again in a little while.*

Passing Mrs. Halvorsen's house, Liza saw movement in the yard. She peeked over to see Mrs. H. getting some gardening done. Rusty gave a friendly bark and all but leapt on the little rotund figure weeding around her rosebushes.

"Well! Who's a big, silly dog?" Mrs. H. asked, giving Rusty the petting he demanded. Then, glancing over her eyeglasses at Liza, the woman added a little cough.

Liza rolled her eyes. "Nice to see you up and around again," she said.

Mrs. H. gave a little shrug of her round

shoulders. "If I leave them alone too long, the weeds would take over the whole yard. Besides, it's not as strenuous as taking that fellow for a walk." She glanced over at Liza's disheveled state.

"Speaking of which," Liza said, trying to unrumple her sweaty sweats, "I've been called away again today. Would it be possible for you to walk Rusty later?"

The little widow lady replied with a beatific smile. "If not me, I'm sure I can get someone to help."

"And speaking of *that,*" Liza said more severely, "I hope you won't drag poor Kevin Shepard over from Killamook again."

"Kevin is such a nice boy," Mrs. Halvorsen replied evasively.

"Yes, I thought so, too — fifteen years ago."

"Why that's right!" Mrs. H.'s expression of surprise was a triumph of amateur acting. "You made such a lovely couple."

"As I said, that was fifteen years ago — and more," Liza said.

"Yes, but he's alone again, and from the looks of things, so are you," Mrs. H. replied.

"Right now, I think that would be borrowing trouble." Liza shook her head. "I don't think you'll find much matchmaking in the Bible."

"You'd be surprised." Mrs. Halvorsen grinned as she returned to her weeding. "Where do you think all those chapters of begats came from?"

Sighing, Liza pulled on Rusty's leash and retreated. "I'd better be getting ready. Tell you what, Mrs. H. — I'll call you when I get back to Portland."

After getting out of the shower and into a suit, Liza did a final makeup check, patting her stomach to keep it from rumbling. *I remembered to feed Rusty and forgot to feed myself,* she thought. A glance at the clock showed that she could still catch a quick breakfast at Ma's Café before heading off to Portland. *Provided I don't dribble on my power suit.*

That plan changed when Liza found Calvin behind the counter at the café, his eyes looking uncannily like the sunny-side-up eggs he was burning. "You look very nice today," he greeted her.

"Thanks, Calvin," she said, dropping onto a stool. "How about a cup of coffee?"

"Soon as I finish this." He scooped up the incinerated eggs with a spatula as gingerly as if they were still in their shells. (As a matter of fact, Liza could see a couple pieces of broken shell, tiny bits of white sticking out from the blackish-brown edges of Cal's concoction.) Cal deposited this burnt offering on two pieces of equally burnt toast, then set the plate down in front of Hank Lonebaugh, who sat between two of the place's long-suffering regulars.

Hank had taken to turning up at Ma's in hopes of catching Liza at breakfast or lunch. This morning though, he was the one who looked caught. His horrified eyes went from the hulking, hungover Cal to his charred short-order masterpiece — and back again. Then, with an audible gulp, Hank picked up his knife and fork and began sawing away.

As Cal turned away to get Liza's coffee, an old codger sitting beside Hank reached up and gave him a comradely pat on the shoulder.

*How nice to see he's finally being accepted by the natives,* Liza thought.

The café door banged open and in strode Lloyd Braeburn. That was a surprise. Braeburn, like most of the California transplants in town, got his caffeine fix at the brand-name latte palace on the other end of Main Street. The locals were just as glad — they tended to loathe the newcomers. Liza always guessed she was a fifty-fifty proposition — a local girl who'd joined the enemy and then came back. At least they didn't ostracize her at Ma's.

Braeburn brushed past Liza's stool as he bellied up to the counter. "I've got a half-finished deck behind my house, and I find you here instead of going to work finishing it up," he said loudly.

"Sorry, Mr. Braeburn," Calvin began. "I can't —"

"If I had a nickel for every time I heard that from a contractor," Braeburn butted in. "I know you small-time guys, always ready to take a vacation as the mood — or the morning after — dictates. If you need coffee that badly, fine. Get a thermos." He banged on the counter. "You're coming up —"

He never got to finish. Calvin whirled around from the coffee urn, Liza's cup in one meaty hand, the other shooting out with unexpected speed to pin Braeburn's fist to the Formica. The startled Californian tried to pull back, but his wrist might as well have been nailed to the surface. Braeburn struggled mightily to get free, but neither Cal — nor the cup of coffee he still held — budged a millimeter.

Liza sat nervously on her stool, staring. The Calvin she'd always known had left the building. Instead, a half-shaved stranger stood glaring at Lloyd Braeburn with bloodshot eyes — a stranger who was twice the Californian's size.

Then, Calvin was back, releasing Braeburn's hand. "Ma's sick," he said mildly. "She says both knees have seized up. Tom Coughlin has the flu, so he can't fill in. It's up to me to mind the fort."

"I — ah, see," Lloyd said, massaging his wrist. "Guess I'll leave you to it."

"Thanks, Mr. Braeburn." Calvin set down Liza's coffee. He looked mild as ever, but she could see the little ripples in the liquid as his hand trembled in reaction.

Liza knocked back her coffee quickly, risking a scorched mouth. Her stomach rumbled again, whether from hunger or protest. *I can always catch something at the airport,* she promised herself.

She paid Cal and headed out of the coffee shop, finding Hank at her elbow as she opened the door. "Does that homicidal maniac come here often to cook?" Hank asked when they were safely outside.

"Cal?" Liza laughed. "He wouldn't hurt a fly."

*Except with his cooking,* she amended silently.

"Yeah. I guess the fly would barely feel it if it were just squashed flat." Hank put one hand to his stomach and the other to his mouth, stifling a burp.

Liza's stomach let out a sympathetic gurgle.

She glanced at her watch. Skipping breakfast had gained her a little time, and seeing Hank reminded her of something else to do before she left — besides, the satellite office of the *Oregon Daily* was right on Liza's route out of town.

Satellite office — that somehow reminded Liza of *The Jetsons,* as if she should be going into orbit when she went to work. Reality was considerably more down to earth. The paper's local offices occupied the second floor of a strip mall near the entrance to the highway. After parking her car, Liza zipped up the stairs at the side of the sporting-goods shop and entered the reception area — two plastic chairs and a plywood partition. Janey Brezinski was on the phone, frantically scribbling away as Liza passed. She made her way through a crowded work space, desks pushed head-to-head, some empty, some with local reporters typing on computer keyboards or staring at their screens.

Beyond was a fishbowl office, the domain of Ava Barnes, Liza's childhood friend, managing editor of the *Oregon Daily* — and Liza's boss.

Knocking on the open door frame, Liza stuck her head into the office. "Oh, Chief," she said, "I've got a bone to pick with you."

"Don't call me Chief," Ava growled, her long, thin face serious as she scanned the sheaf of papers in her hands.

Liza got a little annoyed at being ignored. "I don't mind oversight, but I think it's a bit much when you go poking around in my account in the network."

The papers in Ava's hand flopped down and her mobile features contracted as she stared up at Liza. "What are you talking about?"

"I logged on last night to do a couple of things — got to be out of town again today — and found the account accessed. Figured the boss was looking over my shoulder."

Ava shook her head. "Not me. Jodie was running a temperature — that damned flu. I spent the night being a mommy."

"Then who would have the access?" Liza wanted to know.

"Nobody." Ava frowned, picking up her phone. "Hank, come in here a moment."

Liza stepped aside in the doorway. As Hank approached the boss's office, he looked as if his breakfast was disagreeing even more violently with him. "Problems?" he asked with a slight quaver in his voice.

Liza looked at him with new suspicion. Ava had just denied any cyberspace intruding. But what about the guy who ran the system?

*Maybe I'll log on now and find the screen filled with hearts and flowers signed, "I love you — Hank,"* she thought, wishing now that she'd brought the matter up with her wannabe stalker outside the café.

But he frowned with genuine concern as Liza recounted what happened the previous evening. At least, Liza was reasonably convinced that it was genuine concern. Hank hadn't been a good enough actor to hide his terror in front of Cal or his trepidation at being called to Ava's office. It didn't seem likely he'd be able to hide any computer peccadilloes behind the professional facade he now displayed.

"You didn't give your password to anybody?" His almost-jowls quivered in a dubious frown at Liza's assurances, then he went off somewhere to check the hardware. Liza turned to discover she now had Ava's complete attention. "So, is there a reason why someone would want to hack your files," she asked, "and does it have anything to do with what happened in Santa Barbara?"

After hearing the untold story — and Liza's suspicions — Ava was back into managing editor mode. "And how do you intend to investigate this?"

"From the sudoku end, basically," Liza replied. "Checking the puzzles and trying to see if they actually connect with events — specifically fires — that happened in the real world."

"Okay — doesn't sound all that dangerous." Ava turned to her computer and began working the keyboard, nodding as she looked at the screen. "I'm downloading about three months of sudoku puzzles — surprise, surprise, the *Prospect* is trying to syndicate them. It will take longer to do a search through the archives for stories. How wide do you think we should go?"

"Wide?" Liza echoed. In her world, that usually referred to how many theaters a film would open in.

"Think about it," Ava said. "Three months of fires on the West Coast . . ."

*Or even the Northwest.* Liza imagined the pile of clippings she'd have to go through. "Let's just start with Washington — in fact, the Greater Seattle area."

The search was quick, but the download would still take time. Ava obligingly routed the sudoku files to one of the system printers. When Liza went to pick them up, she encountered Hank. He looked a little mystified. "If we got hacked, it was a slick job. No traces, except that you logged into your account . . . and then you logged into your account." Liza wasn't sure if he was miffed at having his system penetrated, or if he wished he'd tried this particular trick himself. Considering this was Hank, she decided she didn't want to know.

He went off, muttering about firewalls and security systems, while she lugged off paper copies of about ninety puzzles and their solutions.

*Well, now I've got something to read on the plane,* she told herself.

But as she went through the papers on the flight, they turned out to be pretty blah reading. In Liza's professional judgment, it looked as if the *Prospect* was doomed to disappointment trying to syndicate these. Competitors could get pretty much the same thing from Internet sites. The puzzles were nothing to write home about. All of them were asymmetrical, which probably meant they were generated by computer. For a human constructing sudoku, an initial design for the starting clues gives a blueprint to work from. In Liza's opinion, it also helped the sudoku student figure out the puzzle constructor's logic. Will's tournament puzzles had been symmetrical, the bottom halves being mirror images of the top halves. She made a note to include that in her article explaining the basic techniques for solving newspaper sudokus.

Liza picked up one of the *Prospect* puzzles and grimaced. It looked as if it had been just ripped out of the computer and flung in without a second look — a graceless collection of clues, and ridiculously easy to boot. Her trained eye offered solutions wherever she looked.

A glance at the dateline deepened her frown.

*Why would anybody put this in as a Sunday puzzle?* Liza wondered. *Even if there was a horrible deadline crunch, you'd think someone*

| 1 |   | 4 |   |   |   |   |   |   |
|---|---|---|---|---|---|---|---|---|
|   |   |   | 2 | 1 |   |   |   |   |
|   | 9 |   |   | 5 |   | 1 | 3 | 7 |
|   |   |   |   |   |   | 2 | 1 |   |
| 9 | 2 |   |   | 4 |   |   | 5 |   |
|   |   | 6 | 1 |   | 8 |   |   | 9 |
|   | 7 |   |   |   |   |   |   | 6 |
|   |   |   |   | 9 |   |   |   |   |
| 8 |   |   | 6 |   |   | 3 |   | 1 |

*would come up with something better than this.*

Okay, maybe a rank novice would see only the simplicity and miss the sloppiness. Liza picked up another puzzle and quickly found herself slogging away worse than she had at the tournament. If that same novice picked up this puzzle, he or she would have no problem putting it down — probably with great force and far away.

She frowned as she had to force a logic chain to proceed toward a solution. Working from a space that had only two candidates, she chose one value, penciling in more answers to two-candidate spaces — provisional answers, because her initial choice could be wrong. Then she did the same thing, using the other possible number, proceeding in the hope that somewhere, the two chains of logic would intersect, giving her a number somewhere on the puzzle that would be correct either way — a solid start for a valid logic chain.

Not only was that an extremely advanced sudoku technique, it was a time-consuming one, too. *You hardly ever see these in newspaper sudokus. They're more likely to frustrate than entice a casual solver,* she thought, chewing on the end of her pencil as she glanced at the dateline. *And why would you pull a trick like that in a Monday puzzle?*

She'd checked a bunch of solutions but had no real answers by the time her plane landed at LAX. A driver stood holding a sign with her name as she came out of the Jetway, and Liza was whisked to Century City with a minimum of fuss. Even the L.A. traffic cooperated.

The reception area for Markson Associates beat out the *Oregon Daily*'s waiting area by a considerable degree of plushness. But then, the client list was tonier and they often faced longer waits.

A young woman with an unfamiliar face and an air of barely restrained panic manned the reception desk. From the enhanced bustline and collagen lips, this was a Hollywood hanger-on with a name like Bambi who'd hoped for a possible career boost from working at a top publicist's office. The temp had as little acting ability as poor Hank, judging from the tremulous smile painted over her complete terror. *Well, she's obviously met the boss,* Liza thought.

Ysabel Fuentes usually held the front lines for the publicity firm, a smart Latina who knew where most of the bodies were buried. Equally as usual, she'd quit for several days after having a run-in with Michelle until enough time had passed for both sides to cool down a little. In between, a succession of temps would take turns sticking their heads in the lioness's mouth.

"Liza Kelly — I've got a two o'clock with Michelle."

The nervousness quotient rose steeply as the receptionist picked up the phone, spoke briefly, then blinked. "Y-you can go right in."

Liza smiled, understanding the slack jaw and faint voice. This was where one-hit wonders — actors and directors puffed up by studio execs and the media — got a much needed dose of humility, waiting on Michelle.

"I know the way," she said, heading into the inner sanctum.

Michelle sat perched on the front of her desk. With her small size and delicate features, it was no wonder that a smart-ass actor had nicknamed her "Titania" when she'd started out in publicity. Liza wondered whether the guy regretted that now as he played the dinner-theater circuit where Michelle had relentlessly worked to exile him. To Liza, Michelle didn't look like the queen of the fairies — more like a very powerful (possibly malevolent) pixie.

"You made good time," a voice rumbled off to the side.

Liza turned to see Buck Foreman, Michelle's personal investigator, sprawled across the office couch. The physical contrast was striking — Michelle's tiny figure compared to his big, beefy form. Buck looked like the poster boy for police brutality. He'd been a decorated veteran of the LAPD until he had to testify in a high-profile case. A clever defense attorney managed to seize on a taped expletive Foreman had shouted years before in the heat of anger, running it during cross-examination. A neat courtroom ploy, a brief spin on the news cycle — and a little collateral damage: Buck's ruined career.

A friend of a friend had put Buck in contact with Liza. It was too late for damage control, and Buck was being approached for movie roles — generally of the foul-mouthed, racist-cop-from-hell variety. Instead, Michelle had stepped in to help Buck set himself up as a private investigator. Since then, he'd often done work for Markson Associates, which was useful for Michelle. She wouldn't trust most Hollywood private eyes as far as she could throw them.

Liza had never pressed, but she suspected that the two shared a private relationship as well. On the rare occasions when Michelle went incommunicado (as she put it), Buck turned out not to be available, either.

"Hear you just about gave a stroke to the SBPD lead detective." Buck's handsome but heavy features lightened in a grin.

"I think that was more Alvin than me," Liza replied.

"I'm just glad nobody went with this crazy theory you told them," Michelle put in. "Damage control has been difficult enough." She allowed one flash of concern for her friend to pass across her pixie face, gone almost before it registered. Then she went on, business as usual. "There are a lot of media people who are just delighted to see us holding the dirty end of the stick."

By *us,* she meant Markson Associates, of course.

"For now, those snakes are still being careful, contenting themselves with some blind items. So, the big question — do we treat Jenny Robbins as a client, even without a signed contract, or do we cast her as the main suspect?"

Liza just stared. Michelle was obviously at least six moves ahead of her in this mind game.

Michelle's big blue eyes narrowed. "Consider the alternative. If we build Jenny up as innocent, where does that leave you?"

"Has it got to be either-or?" Liza asked. "It could be something unrelated, like a home invasion, or it could tie in with what I was telling the police."

"We're not going with that code thing." Michelle didn't raise her voice, but there was no missing her dead-set opposition.

"Vasquez wouldn't like it," Buck agreed.

"Hell with that," Michelle spat. "*I* don't like it. And, long term, the whole sudoku thing won't help Liza's rep." She glanced at her partner. "You are still part of the firm."

"The sudoku thing may not go away." Liza outlined what she'd learned and suspected since coming up from Santa Barbara.

"We're definitely not going with any of that," Michelle almost glared at Liza. "If you want to play Nancy Drew, don't expect us to back your play."

Michelle frowned. "At this point, we'll stick with the theory that Derrick Robbins was killed by intruder or intruders unknown." She glanced at Buck. "Unless you've got something to say about the disappearing niece."

Foreman reverted to his best cop form, a sort of menacing Joe Friday, as he ran through the results of his background check. "The late Mr. Robbins wasn't necessarily a saint, but he wasn't into anything that should have gotten him killed. As for the girl, since she graduated, she's been renting a house up in the hills. Apparently, she went up to Santa Barbara the afternoon that Derrick went to Orange County. In terms of career, she's been considered for a couple of small roles, and Derrick has been trying to pull together a production for her."

Liza glanced at Michelle. "Quick sidebar. Did you get hold of a copy of Jenny's screen test?"

"I saw it," Michelle admitted. "And the kid does have potential." She raised a warning finger. "If —"

"If she's alive," Buck finished for her. "The search around the house didn't turn up anything. That leaves three possibilities. One, Jenny left before Derrick was murdered. If so, where is she?"

*Where indeed?* Liza wondered.

"Two, the girl discovered Derrick dead and got out of there," Buck went on. "Again, where is she? Vasquez has a solid rep. You can bet he's working hard to find any kind of trail — credit cards, car registrations, BO-LOs, all the usual cop stuff."

"What's the third possibility?" Liza asked.

"That's the one none of us is going to like the answer to," Buck said. "What if Jenny was there when the murder took place? In

143

that case, she's tied to the killer, either as an accomplice . . . or because he took her along."

Neither Liza nor Michelle had anything to say to that.

Buck nodded heavily. "Either way, her future may not be as bright as either of you guys hope."

"So," Michelle said, filling the sudden silence, "we continue with the approach as planned — unknown intruders."

She wasn't being cold-blooded, Liza knew. Michelle would call it being practical. Or was it a case of avoiding what she couldn't control?

The desk phone rang. Michelle snatched it up. "I thought I said no —" She sighed, covered the receiver, and said, "Alden Benedict."

Alden was the new flavor of the decade, apparently — "a real hyphenate," as Michelle would say. Golden boy on the screen, acclaimed director and producer behind the scenes, political activist in his spare time. His last Oscar acceptance came off like a campaign speech for the next election.

When Michelle used the word "hyphenate," though, it didn't mean "actor-writer-producer." She used the term as private code for "pain-in-the-ass."

Listening on the phone, Michelle rolled her eyes, then removed her hand from the receiver. "I'm sure the Caucus of Concerned Voters is an important cause, Alden," she said, "it's just not the cause we've got to concentrate on. That's launching your film. Because if this thing doesn't take off, the caucus and a lot of other people won't be returning your calls next week."

Liza could hear the slam of the cut connection from where she was standing, but Michelle wasn't much moved. "I'll have somebody call later and smooth down his feathers. It's not enough that we got him a Wednesday premiere for this windy epic of his, so he'll have two extra days of box office over other films opening this week. We got him Grauman's Chinese, so he can act like a movie star. But no, we've also got half a dozen pressure groups and action committees trying to ride on his media coattails. You'll have to excuse me."

When Michelle stepped around her desk, she might as well have been stepping into another room. Buck glanced over at Liza. "Want to go out and grab a bite before you head back?"

"I'm trying for a quick turnaround," Liza replied. "After all, your friend Detective Vasquez and his colleagues expect me to be up in Maiden's Bay."

"He's not my friend," Buck said, hiding his eyes behind a pair of mirrored sunglasses. "You take it easy, Liza."

Liza tried to do exactly that on the way home. She needed to. When she'd started out in Hollywood, it was like plugging into a crazy generator that left her almost overcharged. Now, though, even her brief brush with the rat race seemed to have the opposite effect, sucking the energy right out of her.

She sat quietly in the back of the hired car that took her to LAX and was silently glad to find no seatmate on the plane. The return flight passed quickly enough, with Liza trying to get some sort of handle on the mystery sudoku master's style.

By the time she guided her car through the exit for Maiden's Bay, Liza felt as if she'd gotten back on an even keel.

*Damn!* she suddenly thought. *I forgot to call Mrs. H.* Passing the strip mall with the *Oregon Daily* offices reminded her of other obligations. *I'll take care of it all after supper. Damn again!*

Liza realized she had no food in the house except for some frozen solid stuff in the freezer and canned soup. A quick stop at the supermarket fixed that, though. Liza was busy debating the benefits of sautéed versus roasted chicken breasts as she approached her back door.

The kitchen light was on — Mrs. Halvorsen must have come over after all. Juggling packages, Liza reached for the doorknob — and realized something was wrong with this picture. One of the panes of glass was missing.

*This isn't good,* a little voice inside her warned. But Liza couldn't help herself. She peered through.

Her heart lurched. Across the faded linoleum tile of the kitchen floor, Rusty lay sprawled and motionless.

■ ■ ■ ■

# Part Three:
# Forcing the Chain

■ ■ ■ ■

Any sudoku puzzle is, by definition, a chain of logic. Working a difficult puzzle, you may face a situation where you've whittled down the available candidates in a number of spaces to a pair of choices. Unfortunately, in all of these cases, either candidate seems equally valid.

In such a case, you have to act as if either is right. You force the chain by choosing one option and seeing how the rest of the choices play out — how the dominoes fall. Then you do the same thing, using the other available choice as your starting point. As the competing chains of logic twist across the puzzle, you stay on the lookout for a space where, by either line of reasoning, only one candidate is chosen. That space then becomes the solid source for a new chain of logic — after you erase both sets of links leading to that spot. They are only guesswork. Many sudoku mavens suggest using an overlay and special marks to force a chain of logic — otherwise, your puzzle gets very, very messy . . .

    — Excerpt from *Sudo-cues* by Liza K

# 10

Liza was halfway to Mrs. Halvorsen's house before her bag of groceries hit the ground. She dashed for her neighbor's back door and pounded on it.

Mrs. H. opened the door and stared.

"Break-in," Liza gasped. "Rusty —"

"I've got 911 on speed-dial," the older woman said, pulling Liza inside. While her neighbor spoke on the phone, Liza stood staring out the window toward her house. She wanted to go and help Rusty, but if someone was still inside . . .

She couldn't quite get a grip on her thoughts, which seemed to swim over her brain, refusing to mix like oil and water. One set of images showed Hank Lonebaugh breaking in to fill her bedroom with "I Love You" balloons, reducing Rusty to ecstatic immobility through forty-five minutes of belly rubs. Or maybe he used a tiny sleeping pill in a piece of steak. But then the images darkened. Hank was smashing a kitchen chair over the dog.

Somehow in the course of this chain of thought, Hank Lovelorn had morphed into another figure. Liza realized it was the portrait of Neanderthal Man from the old encyclopedia they'd had in the house when she was a kid. But the brutal-looking cave-man had traded in his wildcat skin for a black sweat suit. This was her image of whoever it was who had thrown Derrick Robbins down the mountainside to his death. However, now her brain insisted on creating visions of this hulking character throwing poor Rusty against the wall to lie like a broken toy . . .

The first thing to show that deputies had arrived was a knock at the front door. Liza found herself staring at another old class-mate, Curt Walters. She'd heard he'd become lead deputy in the sheriff's office. He smiled at her expression. "We don't always come up with sirens blaring."

Curt and his partner went up to Liza's back door, their guns drawn. Moments later, Curt was back outside, beckoning. Liza ran over.

"The dog is breathing, but we can't rouse him," Curt reported. "There's nobody else in the house."

*And not much room to hide in,* Liza thought ruefully. Whatever storage space she had was still filled with moving boxes.

"One other thing." Curt conducted her to the corner of the living room where she'd constructed her home office. Now it had been deconstructed, even more messily than Derrick's study had been searched. Liza needed a moment to trace the loose wires by the hutch to where they all should have come together.

"Somebody stole my computer box?" she burst out in disbelief.

"The CPU, they call it," Curt said. "Though why they left the monitor and everything else . . . maybe you spooked them off when you came home."

*Or maybe* . . . Liza's brain just shut down. *Maybe this is getting too weird for me.*

Curt took a statement from Liza and also spent some time with Mrs. Halvorsen. In spite of not getting a call from Liza, the older woman had gone across to feed Rusty and let him out. She was sure she had locked the back door behind her and hadn't heard anything suspicious. "I was just sitting here with the Good Book," she said, patting her old family Bible.

Mrs. H. took Liza by the arm. "I have a spare room upstairs. It's not the Ritz, but

153

you're welcome to use it tonight, or however long you need to."

"No. No. Thank you, but no." Liza stared across at her house. It wasn't much, but she was damned if somebody — Hank, the killer, whoever — was going to scare her out of it.

In the end, Mrs. Halvorsen offered more practical help, rousting the local veterinarian. Curt and his partner were kind enough to get the comatose Rusty off the kitchen floor and into Liza's car.

She brought Rusty to the vet's office and spent a long, anxious chunk of forever in the waiting room. At last, Dr. Prestwick came out, still wiping his hands. "It looks as if someone fed Rusty a fairly massive dose of painkiller wrapped in hamburger," he said. "I think we should keep him overnight, but that will mainly involve Rusty sleeping off the effects. Your dog ought to be fine."

Liza thanked him, breathing a sigh of relief that turned into a yawn of jaw-dislocating proportions.

"You weren't nibbling on any hamburger, too, were you?" Prestwick tried to joke. "I'd be careful driving back home."

Liza was a good girl and didn't wrap her car around any trees. When she pulled up to her house, she found a welcoming committee — a uniformed sheriff's deputy she didn't know.

"Brenna Ross," the young woman introduced herself. "Curt asked me to stay around until you got back. He did a little work —"

Liza noticed that the broken pane had been covered over with a piece of scrap plywood.

"And he wanted you to know that I'd be passing by at various times during the night."

"I appreciate that," Liza began, then broke off as she saw Mrs. H. bustling over from her house.

"Are you sure you wouldn't rather use my guest room?" Mrs. Halvorsen said. "It really wouldn't be any trouble."

"Thanks, Mrs. H., but I prefer my own bed." Liza fought another yawn. "And if I don't get there soon, I'll be falling asleep out here on the porch."

She got rid of the delegation, got the door closed and locked — then turned to the kitchen table, pulled a chair over to the door, and set it under the doorknob.

After doing the same with the front door, Liza dragged herself up the stairs. She didn't even remember getting undressed. By the time her head hit the pillow, she was out like a light.

The next morning was typical Oregon overcast, which suited Liza just fine — she seemed to be operating under a cloud, anyway. Only after she'd already muzzily staggered down to the kitchen had she realized that Rusty wasn't there to be fed.

Looking around, she saw that Curt had swept up the broken glass from the floor — a good thing, considering Liza's bare feet. She also saw that Curt had retrieved the groceries she'd dropped on the way to Mrs. Halvorsen's. Unfortunately, they'd only gotten as far as the kitchen table.

Liza gingerly went through the contents separating them into two piles, Keep and Toss. Meat — toss. Fresh squash — keep. Milk . . .

She hefted the half-gallon container and found it warm. This was not a good sign. Liza knew for a fact that there was no cow juice in the refrigerator. She'd used the last dribble to put some color in her pre-run coffee yesterday morning.

Shaking her head, Liza added the milk to the collection of things to go out. Then she bundled up the Toss pile to join the rest of the trash outside. Then up the stairs for a shower. She needed to be more awake before operating the car. She needed to drive the car to get into town and get some coffee (milk required). And she definitely needed some coffee to face the rest of the day's workload.

Liza came back downstairs toweling her hair, having accomplished step one. She wore jeans, a sweatshirt, and running shoes. After covering her tousled hair with a baseball cap, she pronounced herself sufficiently human-looking for a caffeine fix.

The air was on the chilly side when she stepped out, but the car was nearby. Liza backed down the drive, turned onto the road, and set off for downtown. *You really could have walked down to Ma's,* the voice of her conscience scolded. Between planes and cars, the only exercise she'd gotten was the brief run with Rusty.

*Yeah, and I'll need the car to bring him back. Plus, I want to stop off at the* Oregon Daily *and see what Ava managed to turn up, and talk to my insurance agent.*

She was halfway to downtown, bound up in her internal to-do list, before she noticed the big black SUV following her. That shifted the argument into a whole new direction.

*You're overreacting,* her internal voice chided as Liza took the next left, diverging from her usual route.

The SUV immediately turned to follow.

"Omigod, omigod." Liza's fingers tightened on the wheel.

*It could just be a coincidence.* Liza couldn't help noticing that her internal voice of reason was beginning to sound a little nervous. She sped up and took the next right.

The big black vehicle kept right behind her.

Snatching her cell phone, Liza squinted into her rearview mirror, trying to make out her pursuer's license plate. It wasn't so easy while she was jouncing down the road and the numbers and letters were backward. Then she caught a flash of familiar sandy hair.

Liza jammed on the brakes, nearly getting rear-ended by the behemoth behind her. She stalked over to the driver's-side window of the SUV. "What the hell is the big idea, Kevin?"

"I was about to ask you the same thing." Kevin Shepard stuck his head out. "Why are we on the road to the town dump?"

"I was trying to get you off my tail."

"Fat chance, after what Mrs. H. told me," Kevin looked unrepentant. "I talked to Curt —"

*Sure — they were on the football team*

158

*together.*

"— and when he told me he couldn't leave a deputy here all night, I said I'd take the watch. When you came out, I thought about talking to you, but you didn't look in any mood for conversation. So I figured I'd keep a low profile and stick with you till you got wherever you were going."

"A low profile?" Liza snorted. "I've seen tanks smaller than that thing you're driving."

Kevin shrugged. "Anyway, I'm glad you stopped so I can find out *where* you're going — and if there's a bathroom nearby. Rusty may get away with irrigating the bushes, but I didn't think you or Mrs. H. would appreciate contributions from anyone else."

"Buck — he's an ex-cop friend of my partner's — says that's the worst downside of stakeouts," Liza said. "Especially if you factor in coffee to stay awake."

"So what do the cops do?" Kevin asked.

Liza grinned. "Apparently, a widemouthed jar is part of their standard operating equipment. There's a turnoff ahead that will take us to the *Oregon Daily* offices — unless you want to use the bushes here."

Kevin shook his head. "Nice offer — that's a stand of poison sumac."

They drove to the office. Kevin answered nature's call while Liza riffled through the dauntingly thick file that Ava had left for her at the reception desk. "By the way," Janey the receptionist said, "Ava told me to remind you that your cushion is starting to get thin."

Liza looked up from the archived fire stories. Her cushion referred to the number of columns ready but not published on the *Daily*'s computer network. She'd meant to sort through them the night before last when she discovered the hacker. Obviously, Ava had chosen one for yesterday and today.

*And my computer is gone, so filling up the cushion will be that much harder,* Liza thought. "Will Ava be around in a little bit? I have to talk to her — but after I've had some breakfast."

With that semiappointment set, Liza headed down the stairs to wait for Kevin. She hoped the fresh air would help her wake up.

As she got down to the parking lot, Hank came running straight for her, arms outstretched. "Are you all right? I heard —"

That was as far as he got. A cyclone seemed to make its way down from the stairway, seized Hank, and flung him onto the hood of the SUV. A second later, the cyclone resolved itself into Kevin Shepard. "Stay there if you know what's good for you," he told Hank, his face that of a stone killer.

All of a sudden, Liza remembered stories people told about Kevin's army service, how he'd been some sort of Green Beret or something — the guys who knew how to kill with their bare hands. Right at this moment, she was ready to believe it.

"Kevin!" she yelled. "I know him — he's a friend. We work here at the paper."

Traces of humanity returned to Kevin's face — as well as the beginnings of embarrassment. "I thought —"

"I know what you thought," Liza said. "He's not the guy who broke in last night."

*At least I really, really hope not,* she thought.

Hank sort of flopped around on the hood. "Is it all right now if I —"

Kevin went to help him down from the front of the car.

"I heard about the break-in," Hank wheezed. "Really, I understand."

His eyes told a different story as they flickered between Kevin and Liza. *What kind of people do you know?*

Between Calvin and Kevin in killer mode, Liza didn't know how to answer. When she'd overreacted to Derrick's little "Guess who?" trick, she'd only taken his breath with an elbow. Calvin at the end of his rope had nearly broken Lloyd Braeburn's arm. Now Kevin had looked ready to break Hank's neck.

"Sorry, Hank." That sounded lame even to Liza's ears.

"No, no, it's all right." Hank got himself free of Kevin's supporting arm and began stumbling up the stairs. Obviously, he wanted as much space between them as possible.

"I think both of us really need some coffee," Liza told Kevin. They climbed into his SUV and set off for Ma's Café. Calvin was still working single-handed behind the counter, so they gave him quick orders and found a place to sit.

*The corner booth, our old hangout,* Liza thought as she opened Ava's folder and began spreading out papers. She winced at descriptions of third-degree burns and percentages of victims' bodies damaged. *Not the best appetizer for any meal, much less Calvin's cooking.*

"So what, exactly, are you looking for in that pile?" Kevin asked.

"When Derrick spoke about the coded messages, he mentioned that things happened after they appeared. The one event he told me about involved people being burned."

Kevin looked at the pile of paper. "Well, there's obviously a lot of that going around."

"And there was grumbling involved."

"I expect I'd grumble a fair amount if my home or business burned down."

Liza shook her head. "No, the grumbling took place before the fire. Derrick said it didn't matter how much they'd done, they didn't deserve to burn."

"So maybe it was people warning or protesting about an existing condition." Kevin reached over, took some of the pile, and began riffling, too.

He interrupted his search to go up front and get their breakfast. The bacon was one step short of cinders and the sunny-side-up eggs were runny.

"Just the way I like them," Kevin said, digging in with a piece of toast. The toast, by the way, was just right, and the coffee wasn't bad. As they made their way through the meal, Liza began to feel the earlier cloud around her head dissipating.

Under Kevin's questioning, she explained what had happened in Santa Barbara and what had happened since she'd seen him the other night.

"So you're trying to solve this?" he asked quietly.

Liza shook her head. "I'm trying to make sense of it when it doesn't seem to make sense at all. I mean, what is it with these bad guys? They drop a decent man like Derrick off the side of a mountain with no problem, but they feed Rusty a knockout pill when it would have been just as easy to kill him. They hack into the *Oregon Daily*'s computer network so slickly that our local tech guy — he's the one you terrorized in the parking lot — can't even find traces of it. Then they bust into my house with about as much finesse as a crackhead and steal my computer box."

"CPU," Kevin corrected.

"Whatever," Liza said. "Obviously, I don't know all about computers. But I do know that you only need the hard drive. Why lug off the whole thing?"

"Maybe it's because they are bad *guys* — plural," Kevin suddenly said. "Secret messages being spread through a newspaper . . ."

"Sounds like something out of a comic book," Liza growled.

"That, too," Kevin agreed. "But it also sounds like a group of people, spread out geographically. There may be an evil genius lurking in the center of that network, but he

164

or she may have a hard time finding decent help out at the edges."

# 11

Calvin had a free moment behind the counter and came back to the booth. "Now it *is* just like old times." He beamed, looking at Kevin and Liza. "At least we fixed the rip in the padding back there."

He suddenly got solemn. "I heard there was trouble at your house. Is your dog okay?"

Liza had to laugh. "I love the way people are plugged into the grapevine around here. Calvin, you may have more up-to-date info about Rusty than I do."

Then it was her turn to get serious. "How is Ma doing, Calvin?"

He shrugged. "Not back on her feet yet — her legs won't take it. If she was, you know she'd be back here, while she still has customers." That brought a laugh from some of the regulars. "The doctor is saying that, in another day or two, she should be back."

"And not a moment too soon," one man said, vigorously banging on the bottom of a catsup bottle to get the contents moving. "Calvin, these things are supposed to be hash *browns* — not hash blacks."

A buzzer sounded behind the counter. "Uh-oh, back to the salt mines."

After Calvin left, Liza took a few final bites of breakfast while Kevin continued going through Ava's file. He passed over a pile of paper perhaps a quarter inch thick. "This story got some play up here," he said. "I don't know if you saw it, being farther south."

Liza hesitated for a second. So many of these stories were so sad — people falling asleep with cigarettes, or drunks passing out with cigarettes, or landlords torching buildings. This story seemed to be a road accident. A car had tried to cut off a tanker truck full of gasoline, and the resulting collision had also engulfed another car on the highway. Then it turned out that the second car belonged to a *Seattle Prospect* reporter, and he'd been driving with a full load of passengers, all of them freelance journalists.

The reporter's widow began calling it murder — her husband and his colleagues had been heading off to western Washington State, hoping to do an exposé on militia activity in the high desert. Somebody, she claimed, didn't want that story to appear.

The *Prospect's* coverage of the situation was very brief and stiff, the hallmarks of lawyer-vetted copy, something Liza knew all too well. Competing papers, however, had a field day. Liza was struck by one local columnist's take on the whole situation:

This story has all the elements — splashy death, conspiracy theory, and a hint of scandal — that the *Prospect* would usually take to the bank. Instead, Ward Dexter is trying to sit on the story while every other outlet in town goes into media frenzy mode. I hope old Ward enjoys the hot seat. He's the one who imported this style of "journalism" to Seattle. How nice to see it's come round to bite him in the rear end.

"Looks like this guy is gloating more than grumbling," Liza said. "But then, grumbling — or rather, pointing out the shortcomings of the world in general — is part of the job description for what a reporter does."

"I was thinking that this was the kind of story that would catch your friend's attention," Kevin said.

"Because of the conspiracy theory connection?"

He nodded. "Also because secret messages fit right in with militia types and their conspiracy theory view of the world." He paused. "A militia connection would also explain what we were talking about before — the variable quality of the bad guys. Did you notice that the guy who caused the accident also got killed? That would be typical for those screwups."

Liza frowned. "Whenever I hear about militias, it's always how they're gung-ho types, doing all sorts of survivalist things in their compounds in the high desert."

"Then you must find out who their publicist is," Kevin snorted. "They like to think of themselves as belonging to a secret army. But it's more like *Animal House* — except these frat boys weren't smart enough to get into college."

"And the whole survivalist thing?"

"Oh, they may have a couple of snake eaters around —" Kevin broke off at the look on her face. "That's what the old regular army types called us guys in the Special Forces. Some people from the old outfit might fall in with the militias because of politics, but more likely they're training them for money — and not enjoying it."

Kevin gave her a hard smile. "Most of these militia geniuses are small-town and suburban bigots who get their outdoor skills — and military training — from PlayStation shoot-em-ups."

He shook his head. "The only problem with the secret-message thing — I doubt whether these guys have the brains to solve a sudoku puzzle."

"Well, all they have to do is wait for the solution the next day." Liza suddenly rapped the Formica tabletop in annoyance. "Sometimes I wonder where *my* brains are. We've been looking for fires in real life and haven't even taken a peek at the Bible. Luckily, we've got an expert we can ask."

"Who?" Kevin asked, mystified.

"Mrs. H., of course." Liza dug out her cell phone and gave her neighbor a call. After she explained what they were looking for and why, Mrs. Halvorsen sat in hesitant silence for a moment.

"Fires in the Bible. Well, there was the pillar of fire when the Israelites left Egypt, and the fiery furnace that Shadrach, Meshach, and Abednego got thrown into. I think Matthew's Gospel refers to the fiery furnace, too."

"This has something to do with grumbling," Liza said. "At least that's what my friend said."

"Well, then that last one doesn't count,"

170

Mrs. H. said. "That fiery furnace was reserved for people who didn't believe." The phone was silent for a moment. "I just got my Bible. There's something I remember . . ."

Liza heard the rustle of pages, then Mrs. H. began reading: "And when the people complained, it displeased the Lord: and the Lord heard it; and His anger was kindled; and the fire of the Lord burnt among them, and consumed them that were in the uttermost parts of the camp."

After a brief pause, the woman said, "That's from the book of Numbers, telling about how the Israelites wandered after escaping from Egypt. The exact chapter and verse for what I just read is Numbers, chapter 11, verse 1."

"Numbers?" Liza echoed. "Um — where does that fall in the Bible?"

"It's the fourth book in the Old Testament," Mrs. Halvorsen answered. "Look — my granddaughter got me one of those all-in-one machines. I'll copy the page and fax it to you."

Liza gave her the *Oregon Daily*'s fax number, but her voice was distracted as she thanked her neighbor and hung up.

"What's the matter?" Kevin asked.

"Since I talked with Uncle Jim, I've sort

of been going on the idea that this was a book code — a string of numbers for page, line, and word in the line — hidden in a sudoku puzzle."

"And?"

"Mrs. H. just pointed out to me that there's a different method for finding passages in the Bible — book, chapter, and verse. She just read me something from the book of Numbers —"

"Good choice for a sudoku code," Kevin said with a chuckle.

"It's the fourth book of the Old Testament," Liza said, "so I guess you could represent that with a 4. But it's chapter 11, and in sudoku, the numbers only go up to nine."

"I guess you could put in two numbers that added up to eleven," Kevin suggested.

"Yeah, but that leaves lots of ways to encode book 4, chapter 11, verse 1." Excusing herself, Liza turned to her cell phone again, this time dialing the number Will Singleton had given her for Max Frisch. She was lucky, catching the professor in his office.

"Will's already given me a heads-up call," Professor Frisch said. "Anything I can do for Liza K . . ."

"Here's the situation," Liza said. "We have

a possible Bible citation that might be hidden in some sudoku puzzles." She outlined what Mrs. Halvorsen had told her, along with her own thoughts. "I can get the puzzle solutions to you as soon as I get back to my office," she said. "Do you think you can do some sort of computer search?"

"You said you'd be sending three months' worth of puzzles," Professor Frisch said. "Figure each puzzle has eighteen rows and columns — thirty-six if you read them backward as well . . . That's more than three thousand strings to search through. And with the vague variables you're giving me, we could end up kicking out a bunch of possibly valid results. It won't be like searching for a needle in a haystack — more like looking for a needle in a pincushion."

"I'd like to try the search anyway, if it's okay with you," Liza said.

"I can finagle the computer time," Professor Frisch said with a laugh.

"Thanks." Liza disconnected the call. "Well, so much for the high-tech approach." She told Kevin about Professor Frisch's warnings.

"Well, it's better than nothing," he said. "At least you'll find places to look at more carefully."

"It also means I should get back to the

*Oregon Daily* offices." Liza sighed. "Not only have I got that stuff to send, I should be working on next week's columns."

"I'll see you over there," Kevin said.

"It's not really necessary." Liza shifted in her seat.

"I want to, Liza. Then I'll head back to Killamook." Kevin rose, putting a hand in his pocket, only to be waved off by Calvin. "On the house."

Kevin's SUV shadowed Liza all the way from downtown Maiden's Bay to the strip mall that housed the *Oregon Daily's* offices. *Well, he's close to the highway now,* Liza thought.

She had to hide a smile as Kevin got out of his truck and escorted her up the stairs to the office itself. When Liza caught sight of Janey Brezinski, she looked more like the flustered temp receptionist at Markson Associates than her usual self.

"Oh, uh, Liza —" Janey almost babbled.

"How's that for timing?" The cheerful tone in Ava Barnes's voice was totally synthetic. "We finish the nickel tour, and here's Liza herself!"

Liza turned to look down the hallway — and did her best not to gape at the reason for Ava's false heartiness.

*Looks like Michael's not content with driving*

*me crazy over the phone,* she thought in dismay. *Now he wants to do it face-to-face.*

# 12

Watching the two men walk toward each other, Liza was reminded of the way Rusty acted when he met a strange dog. And, unfortunately, this wasn't the fairly benign, butt-sniffing reaction. Michael's voice held a decided growl as he asked, "Who's your friend, Liza?"

"Oh, we've known Kevin forever," Ava said. "We all went to school together here in Maiden's Bay."

Liza wasn't sure whether this was intended to pour water or oil on the fire.

Michael stuck out his hand. "Hello, Kevin. Michael Langley. Sorry I don't remember you from the wedding, but then, ten years is a long time." His voice was less growly, but still challenging.

Kevin decided not to snap, though. He took Michael's hand, saying, "Sorry, I didn't make the wedding. I was stationed overseas at the time. Nice to meet you, though. And it was good to see you, Liza. As for you, Ava, I still have some issues to thrash out with your advertising people."

"Any time, Kevin," Ava said. "Call me when you get back to your office."

"I'll do that," Kevin said, heading out.

"I've got to get back to business, too," Ava said, striding off to her office. Even Janey suddenly found paperwork to dive into. Liza caught a hint of movement from the corner of her eye. Hank Lonebaugh had been peeking around a corner. But he hurriedly pulled back as Kevin began walking away. *Probably afraid he'll go into a homicidal rage,* she thought.

Left alone with Michael, Liza braced her shoulders. "Let's go to my office, such as it is."

She suspected that before Ava took her aboard the sign on Liza's office probably read, "Supplies." However, it had a door, which allowed her to cut off the newsroom chatter when she was working on a tricky puzzle. Otherwise, the place boasted a work surface, mainly taken up by a computer, a work chair, a bookcase, and a visitor's chair.

"Markson Associates has bigger closets than this," Michael said as he dropped into the chair that Liza indicated.

"Yes, but it also has Michelle."

He sighed. "You know, I came up here to apologize, even though that hasn't exactly worked out so far. I thought this would be better than another telephone call."

"That last one was sort of interesting." Liza couldn't help the dry tone that crept into her voice.

"Dutch courage," Michael confessed. "I still can't speak to that whole *'in vino veritas'* thing, but I can testify that two martinis is lubrication enough to get your foot deep into your mouth." He sighed. "Also, knowing you, I can't imagine you letting this code thing slide. But have you thought about how dangerous this could get?"

"The thought crossed my mind, after my house got broken into," Liza confessed.

Michael nearly shot out of his chair, but restrained himself. "Now if I wanted to start a fight, that would be a great place to fly off the handle," he said. "What exactly have you been doing?"

"I've just been checking into the sudoku end of this," she replied, "and somebody — maybe several somebodies — has been trying either to screw me up or scare me off."

Michael's face tightened as she described the hacking attempt and the break-in. Liza herself stumbled over the story, remembering the strange visions that had plagued her.

Could Hank have been in her house? Why would he steal her computer? He certainly had the technical savvy to get what he wanted out of Liza's machine without taking the whole box.

*Unless he wanted it to look like some nontechnical person had been in there,* that unpleasant voice in the back of her head chimed in.

Still, she found it weirdly more comforting to imagine Hank as the intruder rather than the person or people who had killed Derrick.

She took a deep breath, concentrating on bringing things to a coherent end. At least Michael leaned forward with interest as she talked about her efforts to decode the puzzles.

*Sudoku will get him every time,* she thought.

"You say some of these puzzles are a little weird," Michael said. "What do you mean?"

"I'll show you." Liza switched on her computer and printed out a file. "This is what I call Sudoku 101."

Michael looked over the puzzle. "Symmetrical, and it looks simple. If you just run the rows and columns, the initial clues let you fill a bunch of spaces . . ." His voice trailed off for a moment as he fumbled out a pen. "A 6 goes here . . ."

"Why?" Liza pounced. "There are four empty spaces in that column."

"Well, yeah," Michael said. "But in the top left-hand box, there's only one empty space, and there's a 6 in the column next to it. Down in the bottom left-hand box, there are two empty spaces, but there's a 6 in column three to the right. That eliminates any other 6 in the box. By process of elimination, the empty space in the center box has to be the the 6 for that column."

"Simple — for someone like you, who's trained himself not just to cross-check rows and columns, but to scan boxes and zoom in on situations like that. For a beginner, that relationship isn't so evident. A novice would feel pretty good for spotting that 6.

|   | 1 |   |   |   |   |   | 2 | 7 |
|---|---|---|---|---|---|---|---|---|
|   | 2 |   | 8 | 3 | 1 |   |   |   |
| 6 |   |   |   |   |   |   |   |   |
| 3 | 8 | 1 |   | 4 | 2 |   | 5 |   |
|   |   |   | 1 |   | 5 |   |   |   |
|   | 5 |   | 8 | 6 |   | 9 | 3 | 1 |
|   |   |   |   |   |   |   |   | 9 |
|   |   | 6 | 2 | 7 |   |   | 4 |   |
| 8 | 3 |   |   |   |   |   | 1 |   |

That's actually what my column will be about, dissecting the solution to this puzzle. You know that I rate a puzzle's difficulty based on the number of techniques you need to solve it."

Michael nodded. "The twelve steps to sudoku mastery."

"I changed that — it made sudoku sound like some kind of addiction," Liza said. "Anyway, that technique you just used rates about four or five on the difficulty scale. For an untrained eye, it's probably easier to start crunching the candidates for each box than to try a cross-check like that. With a real starter puzzle — the kind that usually appears on a Monday, you might go as far as naked pairs. What would you make of *this* appearing as a Monday puzzle?"

She handed over one of the out-of-place sudoku. Michael frowned as he looked it over. "Computer-generated, probably. It would give fits to the people who say, 'If it ain't symmetrical, it ain't sudoku.' "

His frown deepened as he began looking for a pencil. "Interesting."

"Because you've got to start listing candidates almost immediately?" Liza asked. "This is like throwing a *London Times* crossword at a rank amateur and saying, 'Good luck, newbie.' "

"Mmm," Michael said, still working the puzzle.

Liza took it out of his hands. "The techniques you'll need to solve that go way up the scale — trust me on that. How about this one?" She dug out one of the puzzles that had annoyed her on the plane ride to L.A. and passed it over.

"It's not symmetrical, but otherwise, this isn't so different from the Sudoku 101 puzzle you showed me —"

"Check the date. That's a Sunday puzzle you've got in your hands."

Michael checked the dateline — and then his datebook. The sudoku spell broken, he frowned in thought. "So these mystery puzzles turn up on the wrong days. Why — besides tormenting the newbies and driving the veteran solvers crazy?"

"That's what I'm wondering," Liza said.

"You've been going on this book-code notion. It can't be that hard to hide a particular string in the solution of a puzzle," Michael mused. "Although, from what you've told me, you're leaning toward biblical citations being hidden instead of individual words."

"I guess so," Liza said. "Does that change anything?" She turned back to the computer. "Speaking of which, I've got a whole bunch of puzzle solutions to e-mail to

182

| 1 |   | 4 |   |   |   |   |   |   |
|---|---|---|---|---|---|---|---|---|
|   |   |   | 2 | 1 |   |   |   |   |
|   | 9 |   |   | 5 |   | 1 | 3 | 7 |
|   |   |   |   |   |   | 2 | 1 |   |
| 9 | 2 |   |   | 4 |   |   | 5 |   |
|   |   | 6 | 1 |   | 8 |   |   | 9 |
|   | 7 |   |   |   |   |   |   | 6 |
|   |   |   |   | 9 |   |   |   |   |
| 8 |   |   | 6 |   |   | 3 |   | 1 |

Professor Frisch."

While she did that, Michael went back to the mystery puzzle she'd taken from him, his frown deepening as his fingers went at a speed freak's pace across the sudoku grid.

"This is almost a joke," he muttered. "Why stick it on a day people would expect a real puzzle?"

Liza heard a quick tap at the door, and Hank poked an apprehensive head in. "Janey said this fax was for you," he said, handing over a piece of paper.

"Thanks, Hank. I'm glad you're here. See all these puzzles?" Liza gestured with her free hand to the three-month collection of sudoku from the *Seattle Prospect*. "Ava downloaded them, but now I have to e-mail them to Dr. Frisch at Coastal University so he can run a search —"

"I could do that," Hank cut in.

"You've got some sort of bulk e-mail?"

"No, I mean I could do the search for you. Frisch may have the big machines, but we've got lots of them. If I could divert —"

"You'd divert the paper's computer network for some personal project?" Ava asked, appearing behind him.

"Why, yes." Hank was still puffing himself up at Liza. Then he realized who was asking. "That is, no. Just that it's, er, possible."

"You keep telling me our network is held together with spit and good luck as it is. Don't go diverting anything. Just get that stuff wherever Liza needs it." Ava walked off down the corridor, and Hank slunk away in the opposite direction.

Liza finally got to read the fax. "This is from my neighbor. It's the passage she read." Liza held out the page. Being copied and then faxed had not done wonders for the old-fashioned printing, but it was still legible. Mrs. H. had circled the passage, printing in bold letters in the margin, "NUM:11:1."

Michael pointed at the notation. "Is that the usual way to give chapter and verse?"

"I'll ask," Liza said, picking up the phone.

"Yes, dear," Mrs. Halvorsen told her, "Bible citations are usually divided by colons, with the name of the particular book abbreviated. Most of those are three-letter abbreviations — GEN, NUM, and so on. Exodus is just two — EX, and Deuteronomy is four — DEUT. But mostly it's three letters in the Old Testament."

Michael's eyes went from the paper in Liza's hand to the puzzle in his as she explained what she'd just heard. "So, some of these numbers might possibly represent letters," he said glumly. "Maybe that would explain the weird puzzles. Fitting something in might require a horrendous set of clues, or ridiculously easy ones."

He scowled, squinting at the finished puzzle he'd just bombed through. "Or could it be something you turn up in the process of solving the stupid things?" Michael rattled the paper as if he expected an answer to fall off into his lap.

"What?" Liza said. " 'The X-wing marks the spot,' or 'Seek the secret Swordfish'?"

"Have you worked all of these through?" Michael asked, putting down the puzzle he'd solved.

"No — although I was starting on the killer ones first." Liza glanced from her computer to the short pile of mystery puzzles. "I thought I might use some of them as the basis for columns — if only as a guide for what to stay away from."

She passed them over to Michael, who riffled through the collection while she tried to work up her notes on the puzzle Will Singleton had given her at the tournament. She didn't get very far, since she spent more time watching Michael's reactions than looking at the screen. In the end, she gave up the pretense of work altogether when Michael held out a puzzle she'd only half finished. "Yeah, that one really annoyed me."

Liza took that one while he took a blank puzzle. The little room filled with a companionable silence, broken only by the *skritch* of pen and pencil points, the occasional wordless murmur of triumph or a *tsk* as a promising line of logic disintegrated.

Liza looked over at Michael. It had been a long time since she'd shared her private vice. He was bent over a puzzle, scowling. *He needs a haircut,* she realized. Michael tended not to notice things like that unless someone — i.e., Liza — reminded him. Well, he obviously hadn't been getting reminders lately.

One of the tousled, unruly dark curls fell across his forehead. Impatiently, he blew up at it as he filled another space.

The action was so Michael — and so use-less — she unconsciously reached out to brush the curl back.

He looked up at her almost in shock, then said, "I've missed this. Maybe I made a mistake."

"In the puzzle?" Liza found her throat had unaccountably gotten very tight around her words.

Michael put the page down. "In a bigger puzzle than this," he said, his voice very low. "I thought I could go off by myself and solve it all, but maybe that was the wrong strategy — the wrong technique." He looked up at Liza, fumbling for sudoku terms to get his feelings across. "Maybe it's not about finishing a puzzle at all, it's the fun of work-ing it out together . . ."

"That's it!" Liza jumped up.

Michael recoiled so fast, he almost fell out of his chair. "I didn't mean —"

"I'm sorry, Michael, it's not something you said . . ." Her face got warm. "Or rather, not exactly the way you meant it. We've been working either on solving the puzzles or their solutions. Maybe that's the wrong strategy."

Michael was having worse trouble switch-ing gears. "Wha-what?"

"I mentioned that there may be a militia connection with this whole code thing, but I didn't mention something Kevin said about those guys. What it boils down to, he doubted that the people waiting for these messages would have the brains to work out the sudoku and get them."

"So the message isn't in the puzzle?" Michael asked in confusion.

"Oh, it's in the puzzle, but it's not about finishing it," Liza said. "What if the message we're looking for is already there — in the clues?"

She scrabbled around for a mystery puzzle they hadn't started solving. "Okay, we've been looking for a string of numbers, thanks to what Uncle Jim told me about book codes. But suppose . . ."

Liza grabbed her pen, outlining the nine boxes in the puzzle with quick bold strokes. "Suppose we break it down this way." She tapped the top three boxes with the pen. "Mrs. H. told us most Old Testament books have three-letter abbreviations. What if the numbers in each box represent or add up to the equivalent of a letter? You know, one is A, two is B . . ."

She looked at the numbers in the first box, a 2 and a 5. "If I add these together, I get seven." She began counting off on her fingers. "A, B, C, D, E, F, G —"

Grabbing a pencil and a piece of paper, Michael began scribbling furiously. "If you do that as twenty-five, it's a Y," he said.

"Could be Genesis, or it could be nothing." Liza put that puzzle down. "We're looking for a puzzle that leads to the book of Numbers."

They went through several puzzles in growing frustration. What happened when a box had four digits? Should they just go with the first two, or one?

"Your pal said these people have simple minds, so let's keep it simple," Michael suggested. "No more than two numbers per box, and we'll read them from left to right."

"Okay," Liza agreed. "And speaking of simple, let's use the puzzle you ripped through at the beginning — the easy one that shouldn't have been easy." She picked up the paper, ruthlessly using a marker to obliterate Michael's solution.

"The first two clues in the first box are right in the first row — a 1 and a 4."

Michael consulted his list. "Fourteen — that's an N."

"Second box, second row — we've got a 2 and 1." Liza peered over Michael's shoulder. "That's a U?"

She quickly moved to the top right box.

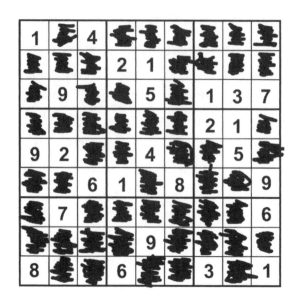

"The first two numbers are in the third row —"

"Am I beginning to detect a pattern here?" Michael asked.

Liza ignored him. "And those numbers are 1 and 3."

"Thirteen — that would make the whole thing N-U-M."

Liza was already searching the next trio of boxes to find the chapter and verse. "Look here — the first two numbers in the next box are in the second row — 9 and 2."

She frowned. "That must be a heck of a long book, with ninety-two chapters."

"It is the Bible, after all." Michael aimed suspicious eyes at the offending numbers. "On the other hand, this is the first time we've seen a high number in the first spot. Suppose that means to add the next one?"

"That would give us eleven." Liza moved on to the next box. "Huh. Here's a difference, too. The first number is a four, but it's not in the leftmost column."

Michael leaned over to look, too. "It's also in the same row as the last clue. If we go down —"

"There's a 1 in the leftmost column," Liza finished for him. "And an 8. That makes eighteen."

"Unless the difference means something," Michael cautioned.

"Like 'skip the next number'? Then we have forty-eight."

"Or maybe it's 'only use the next number' and we have a single 1."

Liza jotted down that possibility and stopped.

"NUM:11:1," Michael muttered in disbelief, staring over her shoulder. "Right in front of us, and pretty damned simple." He hesitated for a second. "Unless we forced the solution. We did make a couple of big jumps along the way."

Liza didn't answer, her eyes riveted on the clues in the middle row's final box. Suddenly, she tore over to her bag, pulling out the fat file she'd left in there.

"What is it?" Michael asked, alarmed.

"Not sure. Gotta see —" She nearly tore through sheets of printout. "The car crash that killed the reporters. I need to see the first story . . . here."

Liza held it up and sucked in her breath. "The newspaper story is dated February sixteen, which means the crash happened the day before. Look in the sixth box on that puzzle and read out the first three numbers."

Michael ran his fingers along the spaces in that box. "That would be 2, 1, and 5."

"Two-one-five, or two-fifteen?" Liza asked with numb lips. "Remind me of the date on the puzzle?"

Michael returned to the puzzle as if the print might bite him. "Sunday, February eleven."

"Just about three months ago, a couple of days before the accident. But it wasn't an accident, was it?" She took a deep breath. "Somebody used this puzzle to order a carload of people killed!"

# 13

"You have a car?" Liza asked, abruptly turning to Michael. "There's a mall about an exit away on the highway — they have a bookstore. We need a Bible."

Michael put a hand in his pocket and came out with car keys. "I'll ask the girl in reception for directions," he said, heading off immediately.

Liza headed in the opposite direction, to Ava's office. She brought the puzzle they'd decoded with her and barged right in. "Check this out, Chief," she told her managing editor before Ava could even say anything.

She showed their solution, then read the passage from the book of Numbers. Finally, she gave Ava the date, then passed over the sheaf of stories about the journalists burning in the car crash.

"So you think that's what happens to people who complain?" Ava asked.

"I'd have thought — hoped — it was just a fluke, except for finding the date," Liza replied. "We've got a bunch of other puzzles in my office, and Michael is off getting a Bible. What we need, though, is research help, someone to connect any messages we find with events out in the real world."

"I can do that, provided you have something," Ava promised. "Or rather, Hank will do it — and he can divert as much computer power as he needs for the job."

"Great — I'll be back as soon as we get anything more." Liza went back to her office and began running through that sheaf of mystery puzzles. Here was G-E-N — maybe it was from the book of Genesis. She frowned in puzzlement when the first three boxes of the next puzzle yielded J-O-S. Was that a book of the Bible?

By the time Michael arrived with a new Bible, Liza had a sheet of paper filled with possible citations. She passed it to him, continuing to work on decoding puzzles.

"Could we switch chairs?" he asked, nodding toward the computer. "I want to type up the citation we end up with."

Liza rose from her seat. "I guess you won't have to worry about this one," she said, waving the puzzle in her hand. "I got the letters B-K-G in the top boxes. Hey, there are probably lots of publicity people who'd love a Gospel according to Burger King, but I don't think —"

"Wait a minute." Michael stood thumbing through pages of his new Bible. "One of the reasons I got this edition was because they have a section on the different abbreviations for biblical books. There isn't a BKG, but there is a book called Second Kings — or 2KG."

"All righty, then." Liza squinted at the other boxes in the puzzle. "Then it's Second Kings, chapter 23, verse 10. And the date is April fourteen."

Michael paged through the Bible, then read, " 'And he defiled Topheth, which is in the valley of the children of Himmon, that no man might make his son or his daughter to pass through the fire to Molech.' "

"Well, that's illuminating," Ava said, appearing in the doorway.

"My grandfather used to swear by Tophet," Michael said. "I wonder if that's connected."

"I wonder if your code breaking is only turning out gibberish." Ava's voice got a bit sharp.

"Let's try another. This is JOS:10:11. 'And when they were fleeing from the children of Israel, and were on the descent of Beth-horon, the Lord cast down upon them great stones from heaven as far as Azeca; and many more were killed with the hailstones than were slain by the swords of the children of Israel.' "

"You're not knocking my socks off here," Ava warned.

Michael turned to the keyboard and began a rapid-fire inputting job. "I'll type these up and print them out, then go on to the others that Liza found."

Ava took the printout and walked off shaking her head.

They continued working up a list of quotations, but even Liza had to admit that their collection was obscure to say the least.

"What were you expecting?" Michael asked. "A Bible quote that said, 'And thou shalt go forth, yea, as far as Santa Barbara, and smite the nosey actor till he dieth a nasty death'?"

"That's not funny —" Liza began, but shut up as Ava again appeared at her door. This time, the managing editor had a slightly shell-shocked expression.

She waved the piece of paper in her hand — the printout Michael had worked up. "That story about stones from the sky? I had Hank do a search on the date you gave me. It didn't turn up hail, but a truckload of farmworkers — illegals — was wiped out that day by a landslide. When the highway patrol investigated, they found the slide had been caused by explosives."

The only noise in the small office was the hum of the computer.

"The other one was a little more difficult for us to get a handle on." Ava was trying hard to stay in her usual impassive managing editor mode. "Finally, Hank ended up doing a search on Molech. Turns out he's an ancient god whose preferred sacrifice was burnt children. That set some new parameters for our search, and we wound up with a right-wing politician commenting on sacrificing children." She took a deep breath. "The story was about an attempt to bomb the stem cell lab at Coastal University. The date of the attempt — April fourteen."

"I'm surprised a story like that didn't get wider coverage," Michael said with a frown.

Ava shrugged. "The bomb didn't actually go off. Apparently, whoever made it messed up the recipe from *The Anarchist's Cookbook*."

"Another job by the lame detachment of the militia," Liza muttered.

"What?"

But Liza waved Ava off. "It doesn't matter."

Michael, meanwhile, printed out his new list. "Maybe this doesn't look so much like gibberish anymore."

Ava snatched it away and raced back to her office. "I'll let you know."

She came back more than an hour later, looking a bit bleary-eyed. "Some of them didn't pan out, but I've got at least three more examples of sabotage and intimidation. Looks like these guys have been busy."

Liza, however, was busy shooing Michael out of her desk chair. "Looks like I have a phone call to make to Santa Barbara."

She managed to find Detective Vasquez at his desk. His greeting wasn't encouraging. "Oh. It's you."

*Well, this time he'll have to listen,* Liza thought. "Detective, I know you thought I was way off base when I talked about Derrick and the whole coded message thing."

"Didn't stop you from telling me then, and I don't think it will stop you now," he grunted.

Liza plowed on. "Detective Vasquez, I think I've managed to decode some of those puzzles. You see, the top three boxes —"

A very audible sigh from the other end warned her this was the wrong approach.

"We've got two manufactured road accidents and a bombing attempt at a research center." Better to go with the more serious incidents, she decided.

"And the Bible told someone to do this?"

"We think it might be several people at least, over a large geographic area," Liza said. "The Bible citations refer to actions that have been planned in advance. You might say they're just the trigger. But there are also dates in the messages. And on those dates, these events took place."

"So you've got some crazy line from the Bible, and a date, and you're saying that because *something* happened on that date, it happened because of a secret message." The detective's voice was like a bucket of ice water right in the face.

"Cause and effect doesn't always work that way. I know. I rubbed my lucky rabbit foot this morning, and I still haven't caught any killers yet today." Vasquez took in a large amount of air and let it out again. "I'll give you another example that's maybe a little closer. My wife is one of those pyramidology nuts. Do you know what that is?"

"Ah — no," Liza said.

"She and a bunch of other people believe that all of history — and the future — is set out in the Great Pyramid of Geezer, or some such. All you have to do is measure along the hallways and whatnot with this thing they call the pyramid inch, and you find out all sorts of amazing things.

"There are these certain marks that were put down in 2141 BC, or so they tell me. Measure down this passageway from there, at one inch for every year, and when you come to the next passage, it's 33 AD — the year of the crucifixion. The next gallery is 1881 pyramid inches long. That was supposed to be the end of the world, but the date came and went, so instead it's just 1914 — a prophecy for the beginning of World War I. Now they have to measure along other hallways to make new discoveries."

The exasperation in the back of the detective's voice came to the foreground now. "But you know what? Every time they announce a prediction, it never happens. Yet they find all sorts of things *after the fact.* You know why? It's nothing to do with mystic powers or secret messages. It's just dumb luck. If you search enough telephone directories and make the calls, you'll probably find someone with my name who'll believe this stuff. But if you want to convince *me,* lady, you'll need more than the luck of the draw. You'll have to predict an event before it happens."

There wasn't much to say after that. Liza hung up the phone. "He says it's just coincidence that these things happened after the puzzles came out. Dumb luck."

"That's just one flatfoot's opinion," Ava responded with a true newsperson's glint in her eye. "Other people might think otherwise when we go to press with this."

Liza thought for a long moment. If the story ran in the newspaper, there was no way she could keep her name out of it. That would mean the end of Liza K's secret identity. Liza Kelly and sudoku would be forever mixed in the public's mind.

*And maybe we'll finally see if Michelle Markson's head really will explode if she gets angry enough,* Liza thought.

On the other hand, maybe revealing what this crazy militia was up to would finally end this . . . what? "Reign of terror" seemed a bit melodramatic, but that's really what it was.

Ava apparently took Liza's silence for assent. "What would we call it?" she said. "Maybe 'Dead Man's Message' — or maybe 'Criminal Code.'"

She was busily sketching out other headline concepts when Liza's computer announced that she had incoming mail.

Liza looked at the garble of letters and numbers that made up the sender's address. Nobody she knew. But the heading was intriguing — "Stop the presses."

She opened the file, but there wasn't any message, except for a box that said, "EX-ECUTING."

Slowly, line by pixelated line, a picture took form. It was sort of blurry, the kind of "photo" that you got by using your cell phone. Even so, she recognized the face of the girl looking fearfully out at her.

"That's Jenny Robbins!" Liza yelled.

Ava and Michael both swung around to stare at the screen. Jenny looked as if she hadn't washed her hair in days. Her features looked pinched, and she was huddled in on herself, either from cold or from fear.

There was no other message, but Liza didn't need to be a puzzle expert to connect the dots. Whoever was behind the militia knew they had gathered information for a story. This was a wordless warning that if they ran with it, Jenny would suffer.

## 14

"Save that picture!" Ava's voice was like a whiplash. She pointed at the screen. "If we can show this to that detective —"

Ava shoved past the gawking Liza, lunging for the keyboard. But before she even touched a key, the screen went blank.

*No, that's not blank,* Liza thought. *It's gone off.*

Judging from the chorus of yells and swearing outside in the newsroom, the problem wasn't just with Liza's machine.

"I think that self-loading attachment had more than a picture," Michael said grimly. "Probably a virus — something really ugly. By the time it's finished, there'll be no trace of that picture — and probably not much left of your network."

Hank Lonebaugh flung himself through Liza's door, his face ashen, his incipient jowls quivering. "What — what did you do?" he yelled. "Whatever this is, it started at your station." He glared at Liza, repeating, "What did you do?"

"I just opened an e-mail," Liza began.

She stopped at the expression on Hank's face. It was the kind of look she'd have used on someone who'd just run over Rusty. No, it was worse — the kind of look reserved for someone who'd run over that cute little toddler who'd fooled with her on the plane to the sudoku tournament.

Ava spoke up. "We got suckered, downloading something we thought was an important clue for a story we're working on."

Liza was silently thankful for Ava's "we." Finding the boss involved, Hank ratcheted back his reaction a bit. "Too late to do anything here — this node will end up shot. I think I caught it early enough so it didn't spread to the rest of the paper's Net."

He didn't say anything to Liza — verbally. But his face, his posture, his whole body language showed that the scales had fallen from his eyes. The woman he'd tried to give his heart to had turned out to be a cybercide. And though he would struggle mightily to save his beloved system, he'd be doing so with a heavy and broken heart.

Liza stifled a sigh of relief as her would-be

stalker went down the hall, back to damage control.

*Guess there really is something to that old saying about clouds and silver linings,* she thought.

"These guys may be hit and miss when it comes to local help, but they're certainly on the cutting edge when it comes to technology." Michael's eyes went from the dead computer to the telephone. "Either they got a hint that we were onto something from the computer searches, or they've got a tap on the telephone and heard Liza talking with Detective Vasquez."

"That's —" Ava began.

"About as crazy as anything in the half-assed scripts I doctor for a living," Michael finished for her. "Funny thing is, I told Liza the exact same thing just a couple of days ago."

Liza's eyes went back to the screen of her disabled computer, trying to call Jenny's picture back from her memory. It had been grainy, kind of flat — a cell phone picture blown up too large. "Did either of you notice anything odd in the background of that photo?" she suddenly asked.

"Odd? Like what?" Ava responded in surprise.

Liza closed her eyes, trying to call up

every detail. "I thought I saw a haystack behind the girl."

"Haystack?" Michael almost yelped out his protest. "I'm pretty sure the background was water, not fields, Liza."

Liza opened her eyes to give him a look. "That's where you find haystacks around here."

"What? Floating around?"

Now Ava started giving him the same look. "It's a local geological formation," she told Michael. "They're rocks that look like giant piles —"

"Of hay, I guess," Michael said.

"Rising up from the water off the shore," Ava finished. She frowned. "So now we know two things about Jenny Robbins. She's still alive, and she's not all that far away."

"I guess it's too much to hope that there's a single formation known as the Haystack," Michael said.

"No, Oregon has a lot of them, up and down the coast," Liza said. "But we know that whoever took her brought her up here."

She turned back to the pile of sudoku puzzles they'd collected. "I want to go over these again, especially the ones from just before Derrick died — and after. There may be some hint about where Jenny was taken."

"I guess I'll have to deal with the madhouse out there." Ava straightened her shoulders and marched out.

"So what are my marching orders, General?" Michael asked with a smile.

"I want you to go to the local library," Liza told him. "Download the latest puzzles from the *Seattle Prospect.*" She gestured at her out-of-commission computer — now just a very large paperweight taking up most of her work space. "Obviously, we won't be getting anything out of this system for a while."

Michael took off, and Liza tried to restore some order to the pile of sudoku, which had grown progressively messier as she'd weeded through it searching for mystery puzzles. She'd already filtered out puzzles which hadn't belonged — brain-busters appearing early in the week. But she'd skipped over the possibility of easy puzzles at the end of the week.

Derrick had been killed either late Saturday night or early Sunday. If some order had been given by puzzle, it should have appeared on Friday or Saturday morning.

Liza got out those puzzles and began decoding. The top line of boxes on the Friday puzzle didn't seem to fit with any abbreviation scheme for biblical books.

Saturday's puzzle yielded the letters

P-R-O. Liza retrieved the Bible and looked through the list of abbreviations. She found that there was a book of Proverbs in the Old Testament. The rest of the citation was chapter 23, verse 13. Thumbing through the pages, Liza found these words: "Withhold not correction from the child: for if thou beatest him with the rod, he shall not die."

She frowned in puzzlement, thinking, *Well, that didn't turn out the way I expected.*

Maybe it was because of Michael's flip comment earlier, but she'd half assumed she'd unearth some kind of fire-and-brimstone exhortation to smite the heathen. "Correction" wasn't even in the same league with her expectations.

And the second part of the verse — "he shall not die" — didn't sound like an order to assassinate someone. *Quite the opposite,* Liza thought. It seemed more as if the order was to administer a beating.

Well, that made a certain kind of sense. Killing Derrick had brought a whole lot of attention in the form of a police investigation — and, Liza had to admit, unwelcome attention from one Liza Kelly and the *Oregon Daily.* If someone had come and quietly put the arm on Derrick the day before, would he even have mentioned his suspicions to Liza on Saturday evening?

The only one who could have answered that question was Derrick Robbins, and Liza wasn't going to hear from him again.

*If I show this to Ava or Michael, they'll find it pretty iffy,* Liza thought. Then she looked to see if there was a hidden date as well. There was — for the very day of the puzzle. So it was a hurry-up job, and given this group's track record, maybe a messed-up job.

She went on to Sunday's puzzle. The letters E, Z, and K showed up in the top three boxes. Quickly checking, Liza found a book of Ezekiel. Looking in the Good Book for chapter 26, verse 5, she found this: "It shall be a place for the spreading of nets in the midst of the sea: for I have spoken it, saith the Lord God: and it shall become a spoil to the nations."

Liza was about to toss that as a dud message when she stopped to check for a hidden date. There was one — again, the same day as the puzzle came out. *Too bad it doesn't seem to make much sense,* Liza thought. Could there be a code inside a code here?

On to Monday's puzzle, a mystery puzzle she hadn't gotten to yet. "J-D-G," she said, examining the top row of boxes. Then she went on to the list of abbreviations. Those letters could stand for the book of Judges.

Okay, chapter 16, verse 29. Opening the Bible to the indicated passage, Liza read: "And Samson took hold of the two middle pillars upon which the house stood, and on which it was borne up, of the one with his right hand, and of the other with his left."

This looked like a quote from a well-known Bible story, but Liza read on just to make sure. Yes, in just a few verses, Samson literally brought down the house, toppling the pillars and dropping the roof of the Philistine temple down to kill thousands.

This doesn't look good, Liza thought. She checked the date — it was today!

Jumping out of her seat, she ran to Ava's office, only to find it empty. She finally tracked down her friend under a desk in the newsroom, deep in conference with Hank. He took one glance at Liza and then buried his head deeper into the router or whatever it was, unwilling to sully his eyes with the sight of a computer killer.

*Maybe someday, when he was a bit calmer, Hank might wonder how an unsolicited e-mail slipped its way past his security protocols, all his antispam and spyware defenses, carrying something that could nuke this whole system,* Liza thought. *Or rather, how someone managed to worm past all that protection with a killer virus. Maybe then Mr. Tech under there wouldn't put all the blame on Liza.*

Till then, though, Liza would be free of his attentions — and free to feel a little guilty. What could she do to make Hank feel a bit better? What he really needed was to be hooked up with someone more in his age and interest range.

*Now, who . . . ?* Liza began running through possibilities, then shook her head. She wasn't the matchmaker type.

But, she realized, she knew someone who was — Mrs. Halvorsen. The only question was, would siccing Mrs. H. on Hank fall under the heading of "doing him a favor" or "getting revenge"?

Ava scooted out from under the desk and looked up at Liza. "Is there something you need?" she asked.

Pulled back to business, Liza nodded. "I just wanted to see if there were any reports about . . . uh . . ." she glanced at Hank's lower half, then decided he was up to his ears in electronics. "Was there anything untoward that happened to a church, or maybe a synagogue, today?"

"Nothing that I've heard about." Ava poked her head up above desk level. "Of course, right now we're kind of reduced to getting our reports from news radio." She turned to one of the reporters, who was keeping up a machine-gun flow of two-finger typing on a laptop computer. "Hey, Murph, you're plugged in with the local pastors. Anything going on with churches or synagogues?"

The heavyset man looked up from his screen. "Nothing I've heard. Should I make some calls?"

"Should he?" Ava asked.

Liza waved the puzzle in her hand. "It was dated today."

Murph made the calls, but ended up shaking his massive head. "Nothing going on."

The look that Ava sent at Liza indicated a serious loss of credibility, so Liza retreated to her office, just in time to meet Michael coming in.

"Here's the *Prospect's* sudoku for today," he said, waving a printout. "At a quick look, it seems pretty difficult for an early-in-the-week puzzle. And the top three boxes give a G-E-N. Even I know the book of Genesis."

Liza stepped over to her desk and all but pounced on the Bible, picking it up and turning pages. "What's the rest of the citation?"

"Chapter 19, verse 24."

It was toward the front of the book — but then, Genesis was the first book of the Bible. Liza read aloud, "Then the Lord rained upon Sodom and upon Gomorrah brimstone and fire from the Lord out of heaven."

Liza's eyes snapped round to Michael. "This is even worse than the last one — is there a date in the sixth box?"

She was hoping there wasn't, that this was just a fluke.

But that hope died when she saw the look on Michael's face. "There is a date," he said tightly. "It's tomorrow."

## 15

"This is terrible!" Liza's voice grew a little wild. Just two puzzles ago, she'd wanted fire and brimstone, something more definitive in the coded quote she suspected was an order to attack Derrick. Now she was afraid she was getting too much. This was the story of Lot, the only just person in the wicked city, warned by angels to escape and never to look back. By the end of chapter 19 of Genesis, the Lord smote several cities, wiping out their whole populations except for Lot's family.

Whatever was being ordered, it probably meant more than attacking a single person, or even a truckload.

*More like a temple full of them,* Liza thought.

"No," Michael argued, "it's not terrible. It's — I was going to say wonderful, but that's not the right word. Let's call it an opportunity, instead. Figure out what this message is about, and you'll be able to predict what the bad guys are going to do. That's what that Vasquez guy wanted, wasn't it? If you could predict something from the code, he'd have to believe you."

He paused for a second. "And I'm betting that you can do exactly that. The bad guys are afraid of you, Liza. They think you can figure this message out. That's why they're threatening Jenny. They want to distract you — or shut you up."

The fear, worry, and responsibility roiling around in Liza's head vented itself in one angry eruption. "Well, thanks, Michael. Don't put any pressure on me or anything."

The weird thing, though, was that she couldn't shake the idea that Michael was right.

It was crazy. For the last two months, she'd been about one step away from being a hermit. She'd come up to Maiden's Bay, trying to clear her mind and create a new life. She'd been up to her neck in sudoku, and even though she'd been working in a newspaper office, nobody could exactly say that she'd been keeping her finger on the pulse of the media. So where did this strange idea come from?

Liza tried to find a logical connection between her recent life and this threat. No actual temples in town. There was a Jewish Center about three exits down the highway and a Hindu or Buddhist temple an exit farther along. *Hmm . . . does the Zen meditation storefront here in the strip mall rate as a temple?*

*Maybe I'm being too literal,* Liza told herself. A temple could mean a house of worship, like a church. Since coming back to Maiden's Bay, she'd attended functions at several local churches — that was part of small-town life.

After a moment's mental straining, she shook her head. No, there wasn't any clue to be found in the pair of musical concerts she'd attended. And while some of the concoctions at the bake sales might seem pretty deadly to a cholesterol-conscious Californian, she couldn't quite tie them into a plot for mass murder.

"What might I know about that would be threatened with fire and brimstone?" she asked aloud, annoyed that the idea still kept niggling at her.

Michael shrugged. "There are a lot of people — and not too far from here — who'd tell you that Hollywood is at least as bad as Sodom and Gomorrah."

"That's true, but — wait a minute." Liza went back to the pile on her work space for the last puzzle she'd decoded. "You weren't here when I did this one." She showed him the citation and got the Bible, reading the quote.

"All the other quotes have been pretty obscure," Michael said. "Then we get two famous Bible stories in a row. Could that mean something?"

"There were two really obscure ones before these." Liza brought him up-to-date on the other messages she'd decoded. "Do they mean something? Do they mean nothing?"

"I don't know," Michael admitted. "But you had a look in your eye when you started talking about Sodom and Gomorrah — and Samson."

"I think they may be connected." Liza said it quickly before she'd have a chance to pick holes in the idea.

"When I saw the quote from the book of Judges, I immediately asked whether anything had happened to a church or temple today. Nothing had. Reading it again . . . well, here — listen."

Turning to the quote again, she read aloud. " 'And Samson took hold of the two middle pillars upon which the house stood, and on which it was borne up, of the one with his right hand, and of the other with his left.' Why did whoever is giving the orders choose that passage, Michael? Why not choose the part where Samson actually brought the temple down?"

"Well, Samson brought the roof down on himself, too. I don't think these guys are suicide attackers."

"Okay," Liza admitted. "That's a point. But here's what I think. In the quote that came out yesterday, Samson is just putting his hands on the pillars — he's *getting ready* to destroy the temple."

"And you say nothing happened today?" Michael scowled in thought. "Of course, this could be like the attempt on the research lab — maybe it just didn't work."

"Or maybe the Samson quote is about getting things ready, and the Sodom and Gomorrah quote is about when it all comes down."

Liza put her hands on her temples, as if she could squeeze whatever was hiding in her brain out into the open. "You don't usually think of a temple in Sodom and Gomorrah," she muttered. "So why do they seem connected to me?"

She tried to clear her mind and try free association, a brainstorming method that Michelle sometimes used. *Michelle — Hollywood — Sodom and Gomorrah — temple*

Her eyes popped open. "Grauman's Chinese Theatre."

"What?" Michael stared at her, completely lost now.

"What's the theater supposed to look like?" Liza asked.

"A Chinese building," Michael replied.

Liza raised a finger. "A Chinese *temple*. And it's on Hollywood Boulevard."

"Downtown Sodom and Gomorrah," Michael agreed.

"And there's a movie premiering there tomorrow. Michelle mentioned it when I met with her down in L.A. The studio is trying to give it a big buildup. That's why they're opening in Grauman's Chinese — and on a Wednesday, hoping to boost the box office. From the way Michelle was talking, they'll need all the help they can get. It's a windy, lefty political epic. And the star is Alden Benedict."

"Ah." Comprehension dawned in Michael's eyes. "A lot of right-wingers would love to see a roof fall on him, followed with lots of fire and brimstone."

Liza tried to pace back and forth in her tiny office, which involved bumping into Michael quite a bit. "It makes sense, doesn't it? The bad guys would be worried that I might make the connection. A couple of months ago, I'd have known all about the premiere."

But she'd only learned about it by dumb luck, because she'd been called down to see Michelle after Derrick's murder.

"It covers both messages," Michael said, doing his best to dodge Liza's pacing form in the cramped quarters. "So where do we go with it?"

"We go to Ava, first."

They found Ava still with Hank, trying to resurrect the dead computer network. He was so busy with some kind of ticklish re-boot that he never noticed Liza and Michael hauling her away from the master computer or whatever it was. At first Ava was too astonished to say anything, but she did begin to protest as they all but frog-marched her to her office.

Her attitude changed radically as Liza showed off the new message Michael had brought in and explained her theory. "I want to get in touch with Detective Vasquez —" Liza began.

"To hell with that," Ava said decisively. "We've got to get down there!" She reached for her phone. "I'll book us on the next flight to LAX —"

Both Ava and Liza stared as Michael

pushed the handset back down. "You don't want to be doing that — at least not on that phone," he warned.

"What are you talking about?" Ava demanded.

"After you began searching for stories to tie in with the coded messages — and Liza called the Santa Barbara police — we suddenly got a message to knock off what we were doing."

"The picture of Jenny," Liza said.

"That suggests the bad guys have some kind of tap on your computer, your phones, or both." Michael dug into his jacket and came out with his cell phone. "You might have better luck with this one."

"Yes and no," Ava grumbled. "I've got our travel agent on speed dial."

She consulted an overflowing Rolodex and dialed a number. "I need three seats on the next plane to Los Angeles," she began.

"Two," Liza interrupted.

This earned her another look from Ava, who put a hand over the mouthpiece. "You have to go, and I'm definitely coming along."

"Me, too," Michael insisted. "After all, it's my phone."

"I need you to stay," Liza told him quietly. "Trust me, it's important."

Michael looked ready to argue, but he glanced at the impatient Ava and shook his head. "All right. I'll trust you."

Ava quickly concluded the phone conversation. "We've got to be in Portland in an hour and a half. I've got a contact in airport security, so I'm hoping we can get aboard with a minimum of fuss."

"Now explain to me why you don't want me along," Michael demanded.

"There's something else that has to be done, something important — something that may be harder than anything we do in L.A. If I'm right about that haystack I saw on the screen, Jenny Robbins is somewhere along the coast up here. You know everything we've discovered from the puzzles, and Kevin Shepard knows the area. Can the two of you work together to find Jenny?"

Michael's face hardened at the mention of Kevin's name, but Liza went on.

"If you're right about the bad guys using her to throw me off their trail — or scare me off — Jenny is in terrible danger. And if Ava and I find anything at Grauman's Chinese — and stop it — Jenny's usefulness as a hostage drops to zero."

Her words evidently took all the wind out of Michael's prepared argument. He opened his mouth, closed it, and then he looked away. "Damn, damn, damn," Michael muttered. "I hate it when you're right. We do need to find Jenny, and I need someone who knows the area."

He gave Liza a lopsided smile. "If this were a movie, that would be the cue for self-sacrificing music to start playing."

"So, we're ready to go?" Ava said.

But Michael held up a hand. "Maybe I've worked on too many cheesy movies, but there's something else to consider. The bad guys probably had a tap on us, but they may actually have somebody in town keeping an eye on you — after all, Liza's house got broken into. Here's what I suggest . . ."

Liza's skin crawled at the thought of hidden eyes watching her as she and Ava came down the outside stairs from the *Daily* offices. They got into Ava's car and got on the highway for an exit, getting off to go to a restaurant called the Famished Farmer.

Growing up in town, she had really only known two places to go out and get a meal. For breakfast, lunch, or a burger and shake before going to the movies, there was Ma's Café. For serious dining — birthdays, anniversaries, going steady — the locals went to Fruit of the Sea in the harbor, a restaurant with seafood fresh off the boat served

223

with an Italian flavor that was exotic enough for Maiden's Bay.

Like everywhere else, the town had moved with the times. A chain coffee palace had opened on the other end of Main Street, and a couple of new restaurants had sprouted up to feed the growing population. This place apparently had a theme. The building was done up with red clapboard to look like a barn, and its sign featured a neon-lit cartoon farmer, knife and fork in hand, licking his lips.

"Michael should be here by now," Ava said. He had left the offices five minutes before they had, heading in the opposite direction as if he were off to the library again.

"The Famished Farmer — is this one of those food by the pound places?" Liza asked, looking around as they entered. The rustic décor continued on the inside, with rough-hewn beams and bales of hay set out for waiting patrons to sit on.

"Actually, it's not too bad," Ava told her. She turned as the hostess came up to them. "We're meeting a friend. Could we just take a quick look in the dining room?"

They went inside to find Michael waiting in a booth that looked remarkably like a cow stall.

*Well, at least there's nothing unpleasant underfoot,* Liza thought, poking a toe at the straw-covered floor.

Michael scooted over as the women were seated and exchanged drink orders for oversized menus. As soon as the hostess left, he and Ava passed their car keys.

"Okay," Ava said, looking at Liza. "Want to check out the ladies' room?"

"With décor like this, I'm thinking something along the lines of an American Gothic outhouse," Liza said.

"Typical L.A. snobbery," Ava said, leading the way. "I guess you'd rather eat in a restaurant shaped like a derby hat."

They reached a door marked with the international sign for females. *At least it doesn't say something like "Heifers,"* Liza thought. Inside, she found fairly generic tile and plumbing fixtures, although the makeup area had some rustic-looking mirrors. *At least the management didn't expect us to sit on more hay bales.*

Ava quickly checked the stalls and announced, "Nobody here." Then she went to the window at the rear of the room and began levering it up.

"How did you know — ?" Liza began.

"Personal experience," Ava replied. "The food here is decent if undistinguished, perfect for blind dates — and it comes complete with an escape route if necessary."

They scrambled through the window, ending up at the side of the faux barn, out of sight from the parking lot. Ava jingled Michael's keys. "Okay. He said he parked about a block and a half away."

The restaurant backed on a residential area, and they faced only a brief walk before they found Michael's rental Lexus. "Well, nobody's trying to stop us." Ava got in and started the car. "Next stop, PDX."

Liza thought of Michael sitting in that ridiculous booth with three drinks scattered on the table. Hopefully, that little deception would keep any watcher hanging around until they were well on their way.

She dug in her bag to bring out Michael's cell phone — something he'd passed over before they even left the office. Luckily, she'd pretty well memorized two of the numbers she intended to call and had a card for the other. No need for speed-dial or memory chips.

Liza dug out Kevin Shepard's card and punched in the number. "Killamook Inn," a perky voice answered.

"Liza Kelly for Kevin Shepard," she said.

Kevin was on almost immediately. "Everything okay, Liza?"

"I need a big favor from you, Kevin," Liza said. "Can you get over to Mrs. Halvorsen's as soon as possible — no questions asked."

"Let me just clear my desk, and I'll be on my way." Kevin rang off.

Liza swiveled round in her seat for a moment to scan the highway behind them, trying to see if anyone was following the car. Ava must have had the same idea in mind. She kept in the right-hand lane, doing a stolid forty-five miles per hour, and every vehicle in sight came zooming past them. Liza turned back to the phone. Her next call was to Mrs. H. *I hope she's not out in the garden —*

Liza's neighbor answered the phone and said she'd be delighted to host the meeting Liza needed. By now, Michael was already on his way there.

The final call was long distance, down to L.A. "Markson Associates," an unfamiliar voice greeted her. Perhaps this voice, too, had once been perky. From the undertone of terror, Liza felt sure she was dealing with another temp fronting Michelle's office.

That was bad enough, but there was worse news ahead. "I'm sorry, Ms. Markson is not available at this time." The voice took on the parrot quality of someone inexpertly reading from a note. "She's in-in — I can't make out the next word."

"Incommunicado," Liza sighed. She knew her partner's style. After laying out the plans for a big event, Michelle often took some time off, leaving her underlings to sweat the details. Her cell would definitely be turned off.

"Communicado?" the voice on the other end asked. "Is that up past Malibu?"

Sighing, Liza left a message for Michelle to call her ASAP and left Michael's cell number.

From the stumbling responses, she wasn't really sure how well the temp was doing taking it down.

*I really have to talk to Michelle — and Ysabel,* Liza thought. *After we get past this.*

After one last look for pursuers, she settled herself as best she could for the ride to Portland and the airport.

■ ■ ■ ■

# PART FOUR:
# SOLUTION SET

■ ■ ■ ■

Even the most difficult sudoku, the ones that require the most advanced techniques, yield their final spaces through application of the simplest methods. That's why, at any point in solving, you want to keep running through the whole hierarchy of techniques that you know.

— Excerpt from *Sudo-cues* by Liza K

## 16

As soon as they were off the plane at LAX, Ava led the way across the terminal to the desk for the car rental company where the *Oregon Daily* had an account. Liza stood outside the rental office for the reception while Ava worked on the receptionist inside, getting them a car. At the moment, Liza wasn't talking but glaring at Michael's cell phone. No, the battery hadn't gone dead — just the brains of the person on the other end.

"What's going on here, Detective Vasquez?" she finally burst out in frustration. "The last time we spoke, you told me I'd have to predict something based on one of the coded messages before I could convince you that there was any connection to those puzzles. Now I've explained what's going to happen and how I figured it out —"

"And you haven't convinced me," Detective Vasquez's brusque voice broke in. "That's a great prediction you made — very exciting, with bombs and everything. Although you didn't mention whether the crime would be committed by a tall, dark, and handsome man —"

"Dammit, Vasquez, this is nothing at all like that, and you know it!"

"How is it different?" Vasquez demanded. "What you're telling me might as well be fortune-telling unless you can show me some solid proof that I can work with."

"That's why I'm coming to you, to try to *get* some proof!" Liza realized people were looking at her and lowered her voice. "What will it take before you admit I was right? A whole theater full of people getting blown up and killed?"

"Hey, I'm listening to you," Vasquez replied. "That's more than anybody on the LAPD would do if you came to them with this story. I'm not going to be the guy they'll make jokes about for believing a bunch of bull."

"But if it's not a bunch of bull, you'll be the guy who got advance warning about a tragedy and did nothing about it."

The detective took a long breath, then let it out — loudly. "You don't get to guilt me, lady. Not till your warning has something more solid than your imagination and wishful thinking."

His cutoff sounded sharp in Liza's ear. A moment later, Ava emerged, car keys in one hand, a bunch of papers in the other. "We now officially have wheels." She paused for a second, taking in Liza's expression. "I'm guessing your call didn't go as well as we hoped."

"He just blew me off, Ava," Liza burst out. "I had the facts down cold and gave it my best shot, and what does he say? That he needs solid proof before he'll do a damned thing."

"That's what we need the police for." Ava rattled her new car keys in annoyance. "I still think we should have gone with plan A."

They'd come up with four plans on the flight to Los Angeles. Plan A, Ava had argued, had the greatest chance of success. They'd just call in a bomb threat for Grauman's Chinese. The police would have to check it out, and when they found confirmation, the *Oregon Daily* could still get a scoop.

Liza had vetoed the idea. Maybe Michael's ideas of taps and spying had made her paranoid, but she feared that the police response to a phoned threat would be too public. The bad guys would be sure to hear about it, either through the news or through their own sources. And then where would Jenny stand?

Liza had felt reasonably confident that after hearing what she had to say, Detective Vasquez would at least unbend enough to have a quiet word with some of his colleagues in L.A. They could institute a discreet search and find proof of the plot with nobody — especially the bad guys — being the wiser. Unfortunately, plan B had not proceeded as she'd hoped.

That led them to plan C, a more unofficial approach to the LAPD. Liza went into the car rental office to see if they had a local telephone directory. They did, and she quickly emerged with the number for Buck Foreman's office.

Buck had a head at least as hard as Detective Vasquez. He certainly hadn't had much to say when Liza brought up the subject of messages in sudoku when she first talked with him and Michelle. Liza wasn't sure how Buck would react at being hit out of the blue with her theory and everything she had to back it up.

Still worse, she was uncomfortably sure that Buck would be reluctant to contact his former colleagues. When he did investigations for Michelle, Liza had often seen Buck put a lot more work into getting information because he refused to plug into the LAPD old-boy system — the old buddies who'd generally turned their backs on him.

I'll just have to convince him. At least he's in town. Maybe if I show him the proof in person, Liza told herself as she punched in the number.

"Come on, come on," she muttered as her call went for three, then four rings. When she finally got her connection, she gave out a louder "Crap!"

"You've gotten the voice mail for Foreman Investigative Services," Buck's recorded voice came over the phone. "Please leave a brief message, including your name and phone number. And remember, even if you don't, I can find you."

"Buck, it's Liza Kelly." Liza then left Michael's cell phone number. "Looks like Derrick was right about those messages in the puzzles. We've connected them with a whole lot of bad stuff that's already gone down, and now we've got a hint of something that's due to happen — at Grauman's Chinese. We're going to be there, so please get in touch with us as soon as possible."

She turned to Ava. "Looks like we're down to plan D."

Plan D was the most difficult of the options they'd come up with — and also the most expensive. The first step involved a detour to Rodeo Drive and the Armani Exchange. Liza's credit card took a major hit, but after they were done, both she and Ava were arrayed in appropriate power out-fits.

"Are you sure about this skirt?" Ava asked with a nervous tug at the hemline.

"Hey, this is L.A., not Portland — much less Maiden's Bay." Liza halted at the leather goods area on their way to the exit. "Well take this, too." She pointed at a portfolio bound in heavy leather.

Soon afterward, Ava carefully made her way through traffic to Hollywood Boule-vard.

"The theater is between Highland and La Brea," Liza directed.

"This place is an absolute madhouse," Ava said with a glance toward the sidewalk. "Where will we find a place to park?"

"There's a mall next to the theater — the Highland Center," Liza said. "It's got a parking garage."

That was an easily solved problem. Her mind was already wrestling with the more difficult challenge — getting them inside Grauman's Chinese.

Ava was not fresh off the turnip truck.

She'd held reporting and editorial jobs on several large metropolitan dailies before coming back to Maiden's Bay. But after parking in the Highland Center, she looked as if she were suffering a bit from sensory overload as they walked out of the mall.

"This place — it looks like the big city in that old silent movie," she said, staring upward at gleaming white walls with a distinctive ornamental frieze at the top.

"*Intolerance*," Liza supplied the title. "Yeah, it's supposed to look like D. W. Griffith's set for Babylon."

"Only in Hollywood," Ava muttered. "Even the shopping centers look like movie sets."

As they came around to Hollywood Boulevard, Ava peered through the smoggy sunshine toward the crew setting up bleachers on the opposite side of the street. "That's for the premiere?"

Liza nodded. "They'll stop traffic along the boulevard between La Brea and Highland — except for the limos, of course. And over there is where they'll keep most of the fans. They tell me when *The Wizard of Oz* opened, there were ten thousand people filling the street. I don't think Alden will be gathering that kind of a crowd."

Ava turned and stopped for a moment to

take in the front of Grauman's Chinese. "I've visited La-la Land often enough but never been here. Now we've got a movie theater that looks like another movie set — the palace of Fu Manchu."

Her eyes went to the two red stone pillars flanking the entryway. "Two columns, holding up that bronze roof to the temple," she said. "Just like in the Samson story. If they came down while people were on the red carpet —" She turned to take in the crowd around them, then did a double take as a guy who looked exactly like Charlie Chaplin walked past, complete with derby, silly mustache, and that odd wobbling gait.

"Toto, we are definitely not in Kansas anymore," Ava said faintly.

Liza did her best to pull her friend back to the practical world. "Any bomb capable of bringing down those pillars would have to be out in the open where anybody could spot it," she said. "Whatever is going on, I expect it has to be happening inside."

They walked across the famous forecourt, decorated with handprints and footprints (and other prints) left in cement by stars over eighty years. Ava slowed down for a second, comparing her shoes to the footprints left by several female screen legends. "Lord, they all seem to have such tiny feet."

"Don't go by that," Liza warned with a grin. "I hear several actresses sweated out cramming their famous tootsies into much smaller shoes so they'd look properly petite."

They reached the entrance, and Liza crisply said to the ticket taker, "Liza Kelly, Markson Associates. Michelle asked Ava and myself to come down for a quick walk-through before the premiere. Is Ray Joyce around?"

Behind the slightly bored facade she projected, Liza's heart was thumping. Ray Joyce was the assistant manager of the theater — at least he had been a couple of months ago, before Liza left town. She'd often dealt with him during premieres, so he'd know her and connect her with Markson Associates. Hopefully, however, he wouldn't be so close that he'd know she was in the process of leaving the company.

The ticket taker beckoned to one of the workers behind the snack bar and dispatched the young woman with a message. A few minutes later, Ray Joyce appeared, his long, thin face lighting up with a smile as he recognized one of his callers. "Liza! Long time no see," he said, shaking hands.

"This is Ava Barnes," Liza did the introductions. "She's new."

"Nice to meet you," Ray said with a smile. "We've laid on the standard spectacle." He glanced at the portfolio Liza carried. "I suppose you know all about the extra flourishes."

"We'll try to keep out of your way," Liza said. "I hope you'll spread the word to the rest of the staff. I don't want them being surprised at where we turn up." She smiled. "This is Ava's first time in the Chinese, and I want to show her some stuff."

Ray glanced at his watch. "The show's letting out in a few minutes. If you like, I could comp you for the backstage tour." He turned to Ava. "But then, Liza knows so much about this place, she could probably do a better tour on her own."

He excused himself, and a few minutes later, the auditorium doors opened and a crowd of people headed for the exits — all except the diehard sightseers who gathered for the tour. "They do this between movie showings," Liza said to her friend. "It actually costs more than a ticket for the film."

Ava pushed open the auditorium door and peered into the large room. "Yikes," she said. "Looks like someone twisted art deco into an oriental fantasy — somebody who really loved red and gold leaf."

The whole interior represented 1920s film

palace décor at its most florid, from the huge electric chandeliers suspended from the ceiling to the bits and pieces of real and faux Chinese artwork embellishing the place. Add in a gift shop, a set of glass cases displaying costumes and other Hollywood artifacts, and the snack concession, and you wound up with a strange conglomeration of tourist destination and museum — which smelled very strangely of roasting popcorn.

"The theater cost two million pre-Depression dollars to build," Liza told Ava. "And the renovation job a couple of years ago cost seven million. They tried to restore some of the original design while also doing some earthquake safety construction."

"There's a nice thought." Ava shuddered. "Lots of pillars against the wall here, too."

"And hopefully, the renovation made it harder for them to fall down," Liza replied. "I still think it's too public. If we believe the coded message, this is something that had to be set up. It would be too conspicuous out in the open."

"So what are we going to do? Peek under every seat?" Ava surveyed the auditorium. "There's a lot of them."

"About 1,500 — or 1,492 to be exact," Liza said. "That's down from some 2,200 when the theater was built. I don't know what that says about the supersizing of American butts, but the seats are a lot more comfortable."

Ava looked over. "You really do know a lot about this place."

"It has a history." Liza shrugged. "And, yeah, I got interested. For instance, in the old days, stars arrived in their limos, but people never saw them leave. There was a secret passage — a tunnel under the street to the Roosevelt Hotel on the other side of Hollywood Boulevard."

Ava's head snapped around. "Maybe we should check there."

"It's been sealed up. The subway line they put under the boulevard went right through the passageway."

"Maybe there is such a thing as knowing too much about a subject," Ava groused.

"Cheer up," Liza responded. "We won't be checking under every seat on our hands and knees." She nodded toward the theater staffers making their way through the theater picking up after the patrons. "Besides, I don't know if anything that would fit under a seat would bring down much in the way of fire and brimstone."

*Bring down.* Liza turned to look up to what would have been the balcony in any other theater.

"Huh," Ava said, following her gaze. "Not much seating up there."

"Originally it just held the projection booth and private boxes — fourteen seats for VIPs," Liza said. "When widescreen movies came in during the fifties, they moved the projectors downstairs and arranged a hospitality setup for the people upstairs — the Cathay Lounge."

She laughed. "Now *that* will become part of 'the good old days.' In restoring the theater, they moved the projection booth back where it used to be, and there's much less space for the celebrities. The VIP lounge is in the sixplex they built next door."

Liza swung the auditorium door open, startling the moviegoers who'd begun lining up outside. She set off across the lobby with Ava trailing behind. "Where are we going?" her friend asked. "The men's room?"

There was a sign for the facilities, but that wasn't Liza's destination. "What we want is over by the manager's office." She pointed to the inconspicuous entrance to a staircase.

As she did, Ray Joyce came out of the office. "I expect you wanted to check the eagle's nest. We were lucky to find a wireless system, connecting the camera up there with the video projector down in front of the auditorium." He walked off as Liza led the way upstairs.

"What was that about?" Ava asked.

"Alden wants to make a speech, but he doesn't want the world to see how short he really is. So he's going to do it on camera up here — that way he can loom larger than life on the screen down there."

Reaching the top of the stairs, she pushed open a door to reveal a private box opera lovers could only dream about. The décor was spanking new and Hollywood plush, although most of the seats had been moved aside to make room for a video camera on a tripod.

"If this area came down, it wouldn't be very good for the people downstairs," Liza said. "But I suspect the main target would be Alden himself."

Stepping back as her friend began to pace back and forth, Ava stumbled, then began hopping around, holding one ankle. "Ouch. What idiot left —"

Liza zipped round and knelt by the black plastic toolbox positioned against the wall. She eased the top open and stared.

No tools, just a wrapped package with an LED timer blinking up at her.

A bomb — and it looked as though it was already armed!

## 17

Liza recoiled so violently, she almost tumbled across the plush carpeting. "We've got to get everybody out of here," she said, scrambling up.

Ava was already opening the door, but she ended up recoiling, too — after bumping off a broad chest in rumpled coveralls.

"You've got to help us!" she began. "There's a bomb —"

"Shut up!" the stranger growled, pushing her back into the box.

He reminded Liza of a wax figure that had been out in the sun too long, with a balding bullet head poking out of a fringe of hair, sloping shoulders, and a thickening middle where the runoff seemed to have collected.

A little belatedly, she also realized he had a small nickel-plated pistol in one hand. The gun looked like a toy, almost lost in the man's meaty hand. But as the muzzle wavered from her to Ava and back again,

Liza didn't feel like laughing.

Obviously, the bomb was no news to this guy. "You two come along with me and keep your mouths shut — understand?" The man sounded as if he were reciting dialog from old gangster movies, the late-night variety he'd probably taken in through a half doze on his La-Z-Boy. He was just a big lug people usually wouldn't notice twice, in a maintenance uniform that was too long for his height and too tight for his circumference. But this was a big lug in over his head. He had prominent, even protuberant eyeballs, and the whites were showing all around as his gaze skittered nervously about.

*This can't be a good sign,* Liza thought. *He doesn't know what to do with us. He's even having trouble figuring out where to —*

"Come on," the maintenance guy said, jerking his head. "We'll go down to the basement and have a talk."

*Right. I'm sure we're in for a cozy chat once he gets us alone.* Liza tightened her hands on the leather portfolio to keep them from shaking.

*There should be people in the lobby,* she told herself. If we ran out the door screaming, what could he do?

*He could shoot you before you even got to*

*the door,* a cold voice warned from some shadowy corner of her mind. She had to admit, their captor looked pretty far gone. *Startle him, and he may well start pulling the trigger.*

However, doing nothing certainly didn't seem likely to extend their life expectancy very far. Liza came to a desperate decision halfway down the stairs. She only wished she'd be able to give Ava more warning.

Swinging around, Liza flung her portfolio into the maintenance man's face, yelling, "Run!"

Ava did her best to comply. But maybe she'd banged her ankle worse than she'd admitted upstairs, maybe her heel caught in the carpeting, or maybe it was simply lousy luck. She only got four more steps before she cried out in pain, her ankle buckling under her.

Liza darted forward, catching her friend before Ava could plummet down the stairway. Instead, she tried to use that momentum to hustle the two of them down the last steps to the landing and out to the lobby.

It wasn't enough. They were slow — too slow.

Glancing back, Liza saw her world shrink to a pair of bulging, panic-stricken eyes — and the muzzle of a pistol.

It was ridiculous, really. That toy gun could only be a .22 caliber. Yet as it pointed at her, the muzzle looked more like an open manhole.

A sudden *bang!* made Liza flinch, sending both her and Ava toppling down to the landing below. Then a large presence shouldered its way past her, and Liza realized the noise had come from the door behind her flying open.

She made a hard landing, hard enough to drive the breath from her. Stars flickered at the edges of her vision, and her eyes squeezed shut as a more deafening noise filled the stairwell — a real gunshot.

When her eyes opened again, she saw a large form bouncing down the stairs — a large form in ill-fitting coveralls. Looming over them on the stairs was the other large figure in a denim jacket and jeans. She recognized the features — large but handsome with a hard expression. That changed slightly as Buck Foreman smiled. "Michelle's got another ex-assistant — your message made no sense at all. Luckily, the message on my machine did. Who is this bird?"

On hearing what Liza and Ava had to report, the hardness came back to Buck's face. He leaned down and hauled up the groggy maintenance man by his collar. "Come on, we have to go outside. My cell phone gets no reception in these old fortresses."

Buck still had some friends on the LAPD. A couple of calls brought a serious response. Soon the big guy was being hustled off downtown, with Liza and Ava going as witnesses, while the bomb squad cleared the building and headed upstairs.

This time when she gave her statement, Liza had an interested and attentive audience. After she finished, she found Buck and Ava waiting for her.

"Leo Carruthers is busy talking his head off," Buck reported.

"Also known as 'big creepy guy with bomb and gun,' " Ava put in.

"From what he said, you were right on the money," Buck said. "Carruthers told his interrogators that he'd get orders through the sudoku puzzles in the *Seattle Prospect*. This looks like a pretty loosely organized group, but one with lots of money behind it. They didn't just use the newspaper. Carruthers said he got a series of single-use cell phones in the mail, each of them programmed with a number. He was supposed to use them to report on the progress of this bomb plot. Usually, it was only when things were about to go down that the go-ahead came through the coded puzzles."

"I wasn't right on the money," Liza said quietly. "Derrick Robbins was."

"There's something else." Ava's voice grew solemn. "Carruthers said he was involved in Derrick's death."

"What?" Liza stared at them, not knowing what to say.

Buck Foreman's face had reverted to its most forbidding cop expression, giving nothing away. "Apparently, it was a hurried job. Leo got it because he lives here in Southern California."

Liza nodded, feeling numb. "He was pretty close to Santa Barbara."

"Leo got a cell phone and called the Captain —"

"The who?"

"The Captain of the Host," Ava said. "Sounds very biblical, doesn't it? Anyway, he seems to be the head wacko, the one who gives the orders in this little conspiracy."

"There was one wrinkle in the coded puzzles that you missed," Buck told her. "The bottom three —" He paused.

"What? Rows? Boxes?"

"It was boxes," Buck said. "Apparently, they held code numbers referring to members who would be involved. Leo had a partner for the visit to Derrick Robbins, a big guy who'd help intimidate him. They went to Derrick's place, and — well, maybe you'd better hear the way he tells it."

Buck brought up a small voice recorder. "They didn't realize I had this on me when they let me into the observation room."

He activated the device, and Liza heard a voice. It was tinier and tinnier coming out of the small speaker, but it was definitely the same voice that had growled at them up in the VIP box — although now it held a distinct whine as well.

"Nothing was supposed to happen. We were just supposed to put the fear of God into this guy." Leo gulped noisily at some sort of drink. "So I remembered something I'd seen in this movie. It had two of the guys from Monty Python, and the babe with the big jugs from *Halloween.*"

"What — ?" Liza began, but Ava shushed her. "I think he means *A Fish Called Wanda.*"

Liza vaguely remembered the movie. Wasn't that where Kevin Kline had held John Cleese out a window by his ankles?

As if on cue, the taped voice said, "We were going to hang him over the side of this terrace place by his ankles. I figured that would put the message across pretty well." Another loud slurp, followed by a half-smothered burp. "Turns out that trick's a lot harder to do in real life. I lost my grip, and the other guy let the actor fall."

Now the whine became even more evident. "So you see, it wasn't my fault. Everything would have been fine if that big jerk hadn't let the actor guy slip through his fingers. Then the girl turned up, and we had to get out of there. So we took her with us. The Captain was pissed about that when he heard, I can tell you for damned sure."

"What happened after that?" another voice came in.

"I keep telling you, I don't know." Carruthers's voice whined on the tape. "I had the task at the theater to take care of. Three months I've been working maintenance there — lousy job. But the Captain figured someday, there would be a movie premiere there, and we could make a statement —"

Buck Foreman cut off the rest of whatever Carruthers had to say. "That's about it. They split up, with the other guy heading back up north with Jenny Robbins."

Liza nodded. "That's what we thought. Do you think he's holding anything back? Could he know where Jenny is being kept?"

Buck's face might not give anything away, but his shrug said a lot. "They didn't even have to sweat anything out of him. This guy is just about gushing information. I think if he knew, he'd be talking."

A familiar face appeared at his elbow — almost literally. Michelle Markson looked like the evilly triumphant pixie queen today. She was all but rubbing her hands together in wicked anticipation.

"Fasten your seat belts," she said. "When this hits the news cycle, we'll be off for a long ride. Network news, the morning shows, late night, the newsmagazine shows, *People, Us* . . . hell, *Time* and *Newsweek*, too!"

"I've got a question," Ava put in crisply. "The only way this story works is if you reveal that Liza Kelly is actually Liza K, the sudoku expert for the *Oregon Daily.* Up to now, you've been a hundred percent against that. Are you changing your mind now?"

Michelle's delicate features congealed into a female version of Buck's cop face. "Who is this person?"

After the introductions and discovering that Ava was in the print media, Michelle grudgingly admitted that the paper had won itself a scoop. "And I guess we do have to go with the sudoku angle as well. Before, it was just some mental equivalent of thumb twiddling. But now —" She made a gesture worthy of a conjurer. "It's solved a murder."

Liza decided this was the time to step in. "Before you go any further with this publicity campaign, you might as well stop here."

Michelle stared at her as if she'd suffered brain damage, not attempted murder. "Whatever do you mean?"

"I'm glad we stopped this bomb plot, but we've got to keep it in the dark," Liza said.

Now even Ava looked ready to kill her. Liza raised both hands. "If the news gets out — if we let it get out — we may as well be signing Jenny Robbins's death warrant. All we know right now is that she's somewhere on the Oregon coast in the hands of a large nut. The head bad guy — this Captain character — already threatened her when it looked likely that we might break the story."

She looked from Ava to Buck to Michelle. "What do you think her life will be worth if this is splashed all over the media?"

After a moment's silence, Michelle spoke, her voice almost compassionate. "Liza, *you've* got to think about this for a moment. I wasn't talking about breaking the story, but how to spin it. Like it or not, this is out already."

Buck nodded, his stone face gone sour. "There are so many glory hounds in this place, they're probably burning out the local cell node, leaking stuff to press people. That's how it is, Liza — you scratch my back, et cetera, et cetera."

"They're right." Ava stretched out a hand to Liza's shoulder. "You've been in the business long enough yourself to know there's no way to keep the wraps on a story like this. Look at it — Hollywood, a movie star almost killed at a world premiere, wacko politics, both right and left, secret messages, revelations, even the Bible. This is guaranteed to sell papers —"

"Or airtime," Michelle put in. "And the media people will all cut one another's throats to get it out first."

"You're right." Liza felt as if they'd all just dropped a heavy stone on her chest. "You're right, dammit, but I don't have to like it. Because it means, unless Michael and Kevin get very, very lucky, that Jenny is dead."

# 18

Kevin Shepard sighed as he cleared the last bits of paperwork from his desk. He'd been letting things slide, spending so much time up in Maiden's Bay lately. Oh, he could kid himself that he was doing stuff for Mrs. Halvorsen, but the real reason was Liza Kelly. All they'd had was a walk in the dark and a breakfast devoted to pretty grim stuff, but he was still willing to get in the car and drive over if Liza asked.

*And that's exactly what I'm doing,* he thought with a rueful smile, wondering what Mrs. Halvorsen would have in store for him when he arrived at her place. *I don't know why she couldn't call me herself. Unless maybe now she's convinced herself she's got laryngitis.*

Driving up Route 101, he debated whether he should be stopping off for gargle or throat spray. That whimsical mood vanished when he saw a strange car in front of the elderly woman's house.

It looked too late model and sporty to belong to old Doc Conyers, the general practitioner who still made house calls around Maiden's Bay. *Maybe it belongs to a visiting nurse,* he thought, almost running up the front porch to ring the doorbell. *Lord, I hope the poor old soul doesn't have something serious.*

Kevin felt a stab of relief when Mrs. H. answered the door herself. Things couldn't be all that bad. He felt a stab of a different sort when Mrs. H. led him into the living room, where Michael Langley sat ensconced (or was that trapped?) in an overstuffed armchair, an old photo album across his lap.

It took him a moment to struggle out of the too-plush upholstery, and when he got to his feet, he took up something suspiciously close to a boxer's stance. But he just held out an envelope, saying, "It's from Liza."

Kevin took the letter and stepped back, using the light coming in through the window as his excuse. By the time he finished reading, he could feel his features tightening into what his old football teammates had called his game face.

He looked up from Liza's words, obviously scrawled in haste, to appraise — well, his rival, he'd have to say. *No use mincing words.*

Michael, interestingly, didn't look much happier — just maybe more resigned.

"You know," Kevin challenged, "from what I saw and heard of you, you weren't all that enthusiastic about what Liza was trying to do."

Michael looked on the brink of a sharp retort, but took a deep breath and throttled back that response. "I also know Liza well enough to figure my chances of stopping her once she's made up her mind."

He glanced at the paper in Kevin's hand. "Since I didn't read that note, I don't know what she told you. We managed to crack the code in those sudoku puzzles — not all that hard, once we figured it out. It led to quotations from the Bible, which turned out to be orders for all sorts of nastiness.

"Liza couldn't convince that cop in Santa Barbara — Vasquez — that there really were messages in the puzzles. The only way she could convince him would be to show him a message that predicted something going down. Then, when we debated going public with all we'd figured out, we got an e-mail to stop us from doing that — a picture of Jenny Robbins, along with a virus that crashed the system at the newspaper."

Michael drew a long, exasperated breath. "Well, we did manage to predict something. Liza believes there's a bomb or something hidden at a big Hollywood premiere." He explained about the two messages they'd decoded, and how Liza had connected them. "I can't say I'm overjoyed at her going to L.A. looking for a bomb, especially when she asked me to stay here. But I promised to help her." He shot Kevin a challenging glance of his own. "Besides, that poor girl is in danger, too."

"So are you two going to work together?" Mrs. H. looked ready to box their ears if they refused.

"I'm sure we'll do whatever we can," Kevin assured her, and she went off to brew some peacemaking tea. He noticed a nearly full china cup sitting beside the chair where Michael had waited.

Kevin turned to his reluctant partner. "Okay, so you saw a picture of Jenny, and Liza's note said it seems to be somewhere along the coast."

Michael nodded. "She told us that she'd spotted a haystack in the background."

"What did it look like?" Kevin frowned at Michael's reaction. "Didn't you see it?"

"I barely got a glimpse," Liza's husband protested. "It was a digital photo, probably downloaded from a cell phone and blown up. Not the clearest thing I ever saw, and it was only on the monitor for seconds. I scarcely saw anything, and then the whole computer network began crapping out."

"So what *did* you see?"

"A good-looking girl, not looking her best. Kind of haggard — pretty much what you might expect after having your uncle killed and then getting kidnapped. She was in jeans and I think a tourist T-shirt, with water and sky behind her. It could have been anywhere on the coast out here north of Santa Monica, except Liza mentioned this haystack thing."

"But you didn't see it? Any kind of rock in the water?" Kevin pressed.

Michael shook his head, looking a bit harassed himself. "You can't expect me to describe something I didn't see. I don't know how Liza could be so sure. For all we know, it could have been the shadow of the picture-taker's finger — these guys aren't too swift — or it could have been a speck of something on the lens."

Kevin shook his head. "Liza knows haystacks. You can't live along the coast here without knowing them."

"Then it's too bad neither Liza nor Ava are here. They might have been useful."

Kevin set his teeth in his lower lip, running over what the other man had told him. "Why a tourist T-shirt?" he suddenly asked.

"What?"

"You said Jenny was wearing a tourist T-shirt. What made you think that?"

Michael shrugged. "It just looked like something you'd pick up on a trip — cheap white cotton. Her arms were crossed, but part of a logo showed. She could have gotten it at school, or at a concert —"

"Or on the way up here with her kidnapper," Kevin cut in. "The Santa Barbara cops would be sure to broadcast a description, including what clothes she was last seen in. Even the most backward bad guy watches enough cop shows to know about that. He probably would have made her change into something he bought along the way."

"Huh. Right." Michael made it sound as if he were annoyed at not having thought of that himself. He narrowed his eyes, as if trying to visualize something right in front of him. Then he closed his eyes entirely. "There was something there, but I can't see it. I just get an impression of very loud yellow, and black."

"Is the black around the yellow?"

"Yeah."

"A very thick outline?"

"Yeah. That's right."

Kevin yanked a pen and a folded envelope out of his breast pocket. Bending over a side table, he sketched a rough outline of an ingot, then covered half of it with his hand before showing it to Michael. "Could it have looked something like this?"

Michael stared for a minute. "What the — ? The answer is yes, except the outline was thicker. What is it?"

Taking his hand away, Kevin revealed the whole picture. "It's a gold bar. The T-shirt shows a whole pile of them, surrounding the town name — Gold Beach. The place is a real cut-rate tourist trap, and that shirt is remarkably cheap, even for Gold Beach."

"So how — ?" Michael began.

Kevin's lips twitched in a sour sort of smile. "Being in the hospitality industry, you learn things. I manage a fairly high-end place. If somebody in one of those T-shirts came in to ask for a room, I'd suspect they couldn't afford to pay for it."

He shook his head. "Well, now it looks as though we have two reasons to believe that Jenny is up here in Oregon, probably some-where along the coast. The problem is figur-ing out where."

Mrs. H. came bustling back with a pot of tea and two cups. "I'll just freshen yours up a little," she told Michael, pouring before he could protest.

Kevin knew better than to refuse. He did his best to look appreciative as he took a sip. "Something more than tea in here," he said.

She nodded over her own cup. "I added a little sachet to the pot. Orange zest and some spices. What do you think?"

"I think you should give me the recipe. We'll sell it at the inn as Oregon Coast Blend."

They shared a smile, then turned back to Michael, who was searching the contents of a large manila envelope. "I brought along the puzzles that came out since Derrick Robbins's death. We figured most of them out, but there's one that made no sense."

He pulled out a sheet and pointed to a cryptic collection of letters and numbers — EZK:26:5.

"This is a message?" Kevin gave Michael a skeptical look.

"It's a passage from the Bible." Mrs. Halvorsen went to the other side of the room and returned lugging a large family Bible. She sat on the sofa, resting the Good Book on her lap while patting the cushions on either side of her for the men to sit. Then, she unerringly paged through the Bible to the book of Ezekiel and the quotation.

" 'It shall be a place for the spreading of nets in the midst of the sea: for I have spoken it, saith the Lord God: and it shall become a spoil to the nations,' " Mrs. H. read aloud.

Kevin glanced over at Michael. "I hope the other messages were less cryptic."

"We were able to connect various events to the others," Michael replied. "But there doesn't seem to be an event here — more like it's describing a place. We're looking for a place on the coast, and this quote mentions the sea. I don't know about the spoil of nations, but does the spreading of nets mean anything locally?"

Kevin shrugged. "Just about every coastal town with a decent harbor has a fishing fleet. They're all out spreading their nets somewhere."

"That's what I thought." Michael's face mirrored Kevin's frustration.

Mrs. H., however, remained silent, bowed over her Bible. She looked up. "I'm sorry, boys, I was reading around that passage. This whole section is held up as an example of Bible prophecy. Ezekiel spoke out against Tyre, which was one of the great trading cities of the Mediterranean. At the time, Tyre was thriving. But two hundred years later, Alexander the Great besieged the city. Now, Tyre had two sections, one on the mainland, the other on an offshore island. Alexander tore down the landward side of the city, literally throwing the rubble into the midst of the sea to create a siege bridge."

"Interesting story," Michael said in a "how exactly does this help us?" tone of voice.

Mrs. Halvorsen didn't listen. "A city thrown in the midst of the sea," she mused — then sat up straight. "Bayocean!"

Kevin stared at her. "That fits, doesn't it?"

"Is this another thing that only locals know?" Michael asked.

"Well, it was before my day," Mrs. H. began.

"About a hundred years ago, give or take," Kevin put in. "A developer picked a spot on the coast here that was going to be the Pacific version of Atlantic City. He built a big hotel, and a resort town grew up around it. That was Bayocean."

"They built some jetties out into the bay, and it changed the currents, or waves, or something," Mrs. Halvorsen picked up the story. "The town was literally wiped off the map — washed away."

"Yikes!" Michael said.

"As I said, this was well before my time," the elderly woman went on. "But I heard about it as a girl. The place wasn't all that far from here . . ."

"Just a long bike ride." Kevin wondered if his face looked as numb as he suddenly felt. "When I was a kid, I used to go out there, exploring for ruins with my best buddy — Cal Burke."

"Ma Burke's son?" Mrs. H. asked. "I hired him once to repair my porch — then I had to hire someone else to fix the repairs." She lowered her voice to a confidential tone. "He drinks, you know."

Kevin nodded, admitting a painful truth. "It happens sometimes, especially if life doesn't turn out the way you expect it to when you're young." He turned to Michael. "Cal was the town's sports hero, a college star — for one semester. Then he wrecked his leg, and he wasn't a hero anymore. He's just sort of limped along —"

"Literally and figuratively, I guess," Michael said.

"Walking wounded," Kevin agreed. From the look on Michael's face, he didn't have to add, *The kind of sidelined, alienated, invisible man who might end up dabbling in radical conspiracies.*

"Maybe we should go have a word with this Cal," Michael suggested. They thanked Mrs. H. for her hospitality, then got into

266

Kevin's SUV.

"We'll try Ma's Café," Kevin said, heading for Main Street. "Cal's mother has been out sick, and he's been filling in."

He still didn't want to believe what he was thinking — that his friend could be mixed up in this nightmarish plot. But things kept coming up to nag at him, like the clumsy break-in at Liza's. Softhearted Cal would never hurt Liza's dog. Kevin suddenly remembered Cal asking anxiously about the mutt. He was also the sort of computer illiterate who'd have to take the whole box if he'd been ordered to get the hard drive.

Kevin's hands tightened on the wheel as he remembered the way Cal had turned up the night he'd been reunited with Liza. *He was right in the shrubbery outside Liza's place — looking for Ma's cat, he said. But he could just as easily have been casing the joint.*

Kevin found a spot on Main Street not far from the café. "So how do we handle this?" Michael asked as they walked up to the door.

"Carefully," Kevin replied. "For one thing, Cal is a friend, and I'm hoping he'll convince us that we're crazy. For another, even though it's years since he attempted a pass rush, Cal is still bigger than both of us together."

But when they got inside, they found Ma Burke back at her post behind the counter. "My legs finally unlocked," she announced. "What can I get you boys?"

"We were actually looking for Cal," Kevin said.

"Calvin? He's probably home in bed," Ma Burke replied. "Been pushing himself too hard, running things here by day and doing his own work at night. When I came in here a while ago, his face looked like two holes poked in a white sheet."

"Well, maybe we'll just stop by and see if he's up," Kevin said. "I've got something that needs doing at the inn."

"Well, I know Calvin will always put you at the top of his list." Then Mrs. Burke waved a finger at them. "Just don't go waking him up, okay?"

"You got it, Ma," Kevin promised as he and Michael left.

But when they got back in the truck, they almost rocketed across town.

The run-down little house where Calvin lived with his mother was dark. Michael took in the sagging porch. "Not exactly the best advertising for the local handyman," he commented.

"That's the least of Cal's troubles." Kevin went up the set of creaking steps and rang the doorbell.

"I don't hear anything," Michael said.

"Probably because it's also on the fritz." Walking carefully on the loose boards, Kevin followed the porch around the side of the house.

Michael trailed behind. "Are you sure — ?"

"Cal's bedroom is over here," Kevin told him. "As long as you don't tell Ma Burke I'm disturbing her boy's slumbers . . ."

Using one knuckle, he rapped on the glass. Then he used his fist on the window frame, finally prying it up and calling inside. "I used to do this often enough, back in the day."

"You don't think he's passed out in there, do you?" Michael asked.

Kevin reached further inside, lighting a lamp. "The layout of this room hasn't changed since he was in high school," he muttered. Glancing around, he shook his head. "Not here, and he's supposed to be dead on his feet. This is not good, Michael. Not good at all."

# 19

Dashing across the porch, Kevin headed back to his SUV.

Michael followed. "You know where he is?"

"I know where to look," Kevin replied. They got in the SUV, turned back onto Main Street, and passed right through town again, this time hitting the underpass beneath the highway to head for the waterfront. Kevin peered up at the sky. "Dusk is coming on. I hope one of the fishermen may still be aboard a boat — and be willing to take us out."

He glanced over at Michael. "Bayocean is located on a spit of land sticking out into the water. Anybody driving — or biking — out onto that peninsula would be spotted immediately. But if we pass in a boat, that might not necessarily make Calvin suspicious."

"You think he's at this Bayocean place?"

Michael asked.

"I'm afraid he is," Kevin admitted. "That's why we need to get somebody —"

"All you need is something that floats," Michael told him. "My dad was a commercial fisherman, and I grew up on boats, right through college. Out before dawn, hauling nets, loading and unloading fish, and then fixing nets and maintaining the goddam boat so we could go out again the next day."

He shot Kevin a not-exactly-humorous grin. "Why do you think I became a freelance writer? You get up late in the morning, and however bad the work gets, it never actually stinks."

Kevin spotted an acquaintance at wharf-side. Mark Robusto was a fisherman who sometimes took guests from the inn out for salmon fishing. Years out on the water had weathered his round face to a sort of reddish mahogany color. Maybe that was why Kevin couldn't make out whether the boat owner was coloring as he heard his client's request. "Most days I'd take you out," Mark said, his brown eyes not meeting Kevin's, "but I really am half dead. I'd probably ram you into the Maiden."

"That's a pretty sweet boat," Michael spoke up. "What is she, a Jacobsen fifty-footer?"

"Fifty-five," Mark replied. "Used to be my father's boat."

"My dad had a Jacobsen, too." As they talked, the two of them gravitated toward the boat. Either Michael knew his stuff or talked a good game, because soon enough they where pulling away from the wharf with Michael at the controls.

"So what is this Maiden I'm supposed to stay away from?" Michael asked as he glanced at the charts.

"Wait till you get to the mouth of the bay — it's pretty hard to miss," Kevin told him.

Before they got to sea, Michael spotted the large haystack right in the middle of the channel. "That is one big mother rock," he said.

"If you squint a little, the additional section on the top looks sort of like a female figure, with the main body of the rock looking like an enormous hoop skirt. When they first sailed round here, sailors called it the Maiden, and the name got stuck on the bay and the town."

"I'd say you'd have to squint a lot," Michael harrumphed. "But after passing the Horn and coming this far north, those sailors probably had only one thing on their minds — and not exactly maidens, I'd imagine."

He took the boat out to sea at a sedate pace, keeping well away from the rock formation. "Very picturesque," he said. "But I'd hate having to find my way in if the weather decided to get rough."

"We've lost some boats here," Kevin admitted. "You can ask Mark about it when we get back."

They had reached the open sea by now. Heavier swells made the deck rise and fall beneath their feet. Kevin ran a finger along the chart. "From here, you want to head south. Just follow the coastline until you see another inlet. Bayocean is — or used to be — on the spit of land to the south of the entrance."

"Okay. Take this for a moment — and don't run into any haystacks while I'm away." Michael left a somewhat worried Kevin at the wheel as he stepped out onto the deck.

The fishing boat cleared the headland south of the entrance to Maiden's Bay. It jutted out into the ocean, the rays of the setting sun creating weird shadows in the craggy rocks of its sides. But there must have been some soil up on top. A lone tree clung at a crazy angle, its branches trailing behind it like a banner — topiary created by the prevailing winds.

Unfortunately, Kevin didn't have much attention for the scenery. He kept looking round for other vessels or any other marine hazards sneaking up on them.

"That's a hell of a view out there," Michael said, returning to the cockpit.

Kevin's response was a stifled sigh of relief to have the supposed seafarer of the crew back near the controls again.

"We're in luck," Michael announced as he took the wheel. "The wind is from the south. Usually, sound travels pretty clearly across water. But this breeze will blow our engine noise away from the ruins of Bayocean. If there is anyone out there, they shouldn't hear us coming until we get fairly close."

"That *is* good." Kevin began rummaging around the cabin. "There ought to be a pair of binoculars somewhere. Then I can keep a watch."

Kevin successfully turned up the binoculars as they proceeded along their southbound course. He stationed himself beside Michael, scanning the horizon as more of the craggy coastline passed beside them.

"We're coming up on the inlet," he announced. "It should be just past this cape

— yes! There's smoke coming up from the spit."

He passed the binoculars to Michael, who took a look. "Yeah, just a thin plume, but definitely smoke. So somebody is there." He glanced at his companion. "The question is, how can we get ashore and find out who it is?"

Cal Burke leaned against a chest-high masonry wall. This corner was all that was left of Bayocean's ritziest hotel. He crossed his arms over his chest, sneaking a worried glance at the girl warming her hands over the small campfire he'd built.

He'd always thought of the ruins of the town as the coolest hideout there could be. That's why he'd told the Captain about it. But the place wasn't just cool — he could feel the dampness from the wall seeping deep into the flesh of his back where it leaned against the salt-stained brick. It wasn't exactly foggy, but a fine mist seemed to hang in the air. Every time he came out here to check on Jenny, Cal's bad leg started to ache about ten minutes after he arrived. By the time he left, his knee had stiffened almost to uselessness.

The place never seemed this cold and soggy when he'd visited it as a kid. Or maybe it's because those days always seemed like summer.

Today, dealing with real-world weather, he had to admit that the corner of a wrecked building, open to the sky and right beside the water, wasn't such a good choice for a campout. For one thing, it wasn't healthy. Even though Cal set up a small pup tent for Jenny Robbins, she'd developed a worrying cough.

*Yeah, maybe that happens, lying around all day tied up.* But he couldn't let her just hang around when he had to work all day. She'd get away.

Cal forced back a sudden gust of wild laughter at his worrying over Jenny's health . . . after the Captain had ordered him to kill her.

Cal had thrown the cell phone out into the ocean as far as he could. But that didn't solve the problem.

When he'd hooked up with the Captain, Cal thought he'd joined a fight he could believe in. It wasn't about saving a country or the world. Cal was saving the people around him — the people of Maiden's Bay — from turning into Californians. Oh, people in town bitched and moaned about the newcomers turning up and waving their money around. But they were becoming more and more like those people every day — take Mr. Schenck, of Schenck's Motors. He'd given Cal a car to go off to college. But after Cal blew out his knee and came home, Mr. Schenck was there, taking the car back — acting like a Californian.

Stumbling across the Captain's movement while surfing the Net, Cal had envisioned himself sticking it to government types, to office people like those smug bastards at the college, to people who paid a bazillion dollars for a house, then nickeled and dimed the person they hired to fix it — treating him like dirt.

Instead, he ended up being ordered to kill a girl. If things had gone differently, he could imagine having a daughter like Jenny. How could he kill her?

Everything had just gone to hell since he saw that coded message in the paper. A phone arrived in the mail, and that Carruthers jackass had called with plans to lean on this dumb Hollywood guy who was sticking his nose into the Captain's business.

He thought Carruthers knew what he was doing, but he began to wonder when the guy told him his real name. Then he said they could use an idiot trick he'd seen in a movie — holding the guy over the end of that mountainside terrace. Carruthers fumbled the hold, and then Cal's knee had given out. He nearly got pulled through those planters, trying to keep hold of the actor guy, only to lose him in the end. Carruthers had been in a panic to get them out of there. He'd actually pulled a gun when they bumped into the girl coming home.

Cal had had enough. He'd flatly told Carruthers the girl wasn't going to die, and he was big enough to make it stick. Carruthers had used one of the special cell phones to bitch to the Captain, but they'd been tasked to keep Jenny as a hostage. Cal had been glad when Carruthers was called away — he hadn't liked the way the guy had looked at Jenny.

At first he'd been told to move the girl and hold her up here on the coast. Then, suddenly, he'd gotten a call on the cell phone, a bossy voice telling him Jenny was no longer useful as a hostage — and telling him to eliminate her.

Cal said no and flung the phone away. But he'd spent the time since just sort of moving in place. He didn't want to hurt Jenny. But if he just let her go, there'd be a kidnapping charge — not to mention murder. For about the fiftieth time, he tried to pull his thoughts together, to figure some way to explain things to Jenny. *If I could just get her to promise —*

His fumbling thoughts were shattered by the sound of a boat engine. Calvin jumped over to the fire, kicking sand over it. "You got to get down," he told Jenny almost apologetically, pushing her behind the wall.

He yanked up the binoculars hanging from his neck. Okay. It was just a fishing boat heading into the bay. Two people in the wheelhouse — he couldn't make them out well in the gathering dark.

Cal breathed a sigh of relief as the engine sounds grew more distant. He turned to help Jenny up. "I'm sorry about that. Hell, I'm sorry about everything. It wasn't supposed to happen this way, believe me —"

Another approaching engine shut him up. Cal peered over the wall. This time the noise was coming from land. He saw a pair of car headlights bouncing over the dunes toward the tip of the spit. The car pulled up near the wall. It was a rental model from the Portland airport, obviously driven hard since it had gone off the road.

The door swung open, and a short little guy with thinning blond hair came out. He carried a five-cell flashlight in one hand. The beam glinted off his glasses as he reached to push them back up his nose.

"Burke!" the man called. His voice

sounded like the one that had barked in his ear over the phone. "Are you there? It's the Captain."

This was the Captain? Calvin stepped around the clump of dune grass that clung round the ruined wall. "I'm here."

"And the girl?"

Jenny joined Cal. "H-hello?"

The Captain began shouting, calling Jenny dirty names — Cal, too, as well as Leo Carruthers, Derrick Robbins, even Liza Kelly. When that ran down, the man's voice was still quivering with fury as he said, "I told you to dispose of her. I came to check on it, since you apparently lacked the brains to follow a simple order."

He shook his head, light glinting off his eyeglasses again. "Just another faulty tool, like so many have failed me. Well, that can be remedied. I can find new followers — efficient ones — after I've moved on.

"But first, I need to deal with some loose ends. The Captain may disappear, but those who tried to cross him should know that he means business." Reaching into a pocket of the baggy jacket he wore, the man pulled out an automatic pistol.

"Hey," Cal said, moving between the man — the Captain? — and Jenny.

"What a gentleman." The look on the

stranger's pudgy face reminded Cal of some of the people he'd done work for — people who'd stiffed him, claiming the job wasn't done right. "Or are you getting some, Calvin? Is she trying to lie back and earn her freedom?"

"That's not nice." Cal took a step forward.

"It doesn't matter," the Captain's voice grew hard. "Ladies don't have to go first."

The guy began to raise his gun hand, and Cal made his move. It was just like the old days on the field. The other side could never believe a guy his size could move so fast. He was almost on top of the Captain — or whoever — by the time he got his gun up.

Cal saw a flash. Something pounded the right side of his chest and a volcano seemed to erupt there, even as a roar blasted his ears.

*I been shot. Jeeze, this is worse than when I did in my knee,* he thought. The force twisted him around, but he still managed to fling out his left arm. His fist made a satisfying contact with the other man's head, even though the shock made the pain in his chest worse.

Cal managed to grab onto the other man's coat, so he'd fall after him — across him. Landing brought new flames to his shoulder and blossoms of flame across his vision. But if he could hold this guy down —

"Run," he tried to shout to Jenny, but his voice came out more as a croak.

The man under him was trying to get loose, and there was no more Cal could do. Then, suddenly, there were two more men joining the struggle, holding the Captain down.

*As long as Jenny is all right,* Cal thought.

The darkness that had edged his vision expanded until it swallowed everything up.

# 20

If the aftermath of the bombing attempt at Grauman's Chinese was an example of how the LAPD reacted to averted crimes, Liza didn't want to see how they dealt with the unsolved variety. By the time she finally got finished with the bureaucratic nonsense and flew back to Oregon, night had fallen.

At least she and Ava had heard the good news before leaving police headquarters. While she was signing her official statement, a detective came in, announcing that Jenny Robbins had been rescued and the mysterious Captain had been caught.

"The guy had a suitcase full of money and papers for four different identities," the detective told his colleagues. "He was all ready to get into the wind, but he still had his real ID in his wallet — *Abner Oscar Galt.*

"Turns out Abner was one of those computer whiz kids who made a bundle during the dotcom days. He started a small company that got bought up by a bigger company for mucho dinero. It should have been enough to set him up for the rest of his life. But when the bubble burst and times got tough, Abner got pretty crazy over parting with any of his capital gains — especially for taxes."

"How did he go from nerd to Captain?" one of the detectives working with Liza asked.

The first detective shrugged. "Looks like he got real busy on the keyboard, writing for *Soldier of Fortune*-type magazines and ranting online — blogs, chat rooms, newsgroups, you name it. He had a whole bunch of people listening to him, and found a few who were willing to go to the next level. The problem was, most of the losers he recruited fu—" The policeman looked at his female, non-cop audience. "er, screwed up, so Cap'n Abner figured he'd move along and try again somewhere else. But he had another problem. He began to believe all this tough-guy nonsense he was spouting, taking his act a little too seriously. So he decided to act like a hard man and kill off that girl."

That bit of bravado had proven to be the Captain's — or rather, Abner's — downfall. Kevin and Michael had managed to stop him, and the man's crazy conspiracy had ended.

Liza was glad it was all over and even gladder to be getting home. She and Ava had a moment of doubt and fear at the Portland airport. In their rush to catch the plane to L.A. and reach the Chinese Theatre, neither of them had paid much attention to exactly where they'd parked. Now, facing ranks of cars in the darkness, Liza admitted she couldn't even remember what kind of car Michael had rented.

"A Lexus?" Ava guessed, then nodded in triumph as she dug out the keys. "It comes with that doohickey."

At last they spotted the flashing light and sounding horn. "Hopefully we didn't wear out the battery," Ava tried to joke. She was a little hoarse, having spent considerable time on the phone with the head office of the *Oregon Daily,* relating her first-person experience averting the bomb plot. Liza was also due to come in for considerable ink, and Liza K was definitely going to be outed.

Michelle had been surprisingly mellow about this development. Or rather, as she put it, "Publicist who develops and writes about geeky puzzles — weirdo. Publicist who decodes brain-busting puzzles to save a theater full of people — hero. In fact, the only drawback I detect with this whole thing is that you saved Alden Benedict doing it."

She glanced at her partner. "See the difference, Liza?"

Liza had to admit she did. "I guess that's why you're the boss, Boss," she said.

"Here's another reason." Michelle handed Liza a thick envelope. "I zipped back to the office for this. It's a contract for Jenny Robbins, along with advice on representation if she hasn't got any yet."

"Michelle, the girl is still in the hospital," Liza began.

"Like that would stop any of the barracudas in The Business," Michelle scoffed. "Just take it along and see what happens."

So, Liza had the envelope with her as she and Ava arrived at County Hospital. "My people tell me that Jenny is in good condition," Ava reported. "They just have her under observation after being stuck out in the open for so long."

She grinned. "With luck, I may even get a quick interview with her."

"I wouldn't bet on it," Liza warned. As they came inside, she was a little surprised to see two doctors in surgical scrubs sitting in the waiting area. Then she looked past the costumes to the men wearing them as they rose and came toward her.

"What are you two doing in that getup?" she demanded of Michael and Kevin.

"They gave us these after they brought us to the hospital," Kevin replied. "Our clothes were kind of soaked."

Michael nodded. "See, I brought our boat past this ruined place —"

"Bayocean," Kevin put in.

Liza nodded in recognition.

"Then I cut the engine and we slipped into the water, swimming to the tip of this point, or sand spit, whatever you people call them up here."

"The real doctors wanted to check us out after taking a dip in the Pacific at this time of year," Kevin said.

"I understand they have this thing in Brooklyn called the Polar Bear Club." Michael gave a very convincing shiver. "Maybe we can start a local affiliate."

Kevin took up the story. "Anyway, we came crawling up on the ruins — what's left of the old hotel cellar."

"Getting sand in places I don't think I'm allowed to tell you about anymore," Michael added.

"While we were doing that, a car came from the landward end," Kevin went on. "This Captain guy gets out — let me tell

287

you, he didn't look like any captain I ever saw."

Michael nodded. "When they do the movie version, they should look at Jason Alexander for the part."

"We had a ringside seat hearing this guy admit to conspiracy to murder," Kevin picked up the story again. "Then it got really ugly. The Captain pulled a gun."

"He was going to shoot Jenny Robbins, but Calvin stopped him," Michael said. "Damnedest thing I ever saw, him charging the guy's gun. And even though he was fatally shot, he still managed to deck the other guy."

"And when he fell, he pinned the Captain's gun hand," Kevin finished. "The guy was fighting deadweight trying to get it loose when we nailed him."

He shook his head. "Cal's life took a left turn pretty early, and he made a lot of bad choices. But the last thing he did — he was a hero."

"He saved the girl," Michael said, "and he clocked the bad guy. Maybe that was the best way he could go." He shook his way out of that somber mood, going for practical instead. "Visiting hours are over, but I understand Jenny was asking for you. Just talk to the people at reception."

The hospital staff greeted Liza warmly. Ava got a less friendly reaction. She was recognized as a newspaper person, and it was all Liza could do to keep her from being exiled to the three-ring media circus going on in the parking lot.

"So much for the idea of an interview," Ava muttered as she went back to join Kevin and Michael.

Frankly, Liza didn't much care. The only news she was interested in right now was about Jenny's condition.

"We're treating it as a case of exposure," the nurse leading Liza to Jenny's room explained. "Hypothermia — and don't be surprised at the oxygen mask. There's a possibility of pneumonia."

Liza was glad she'd gotten the warning before she stepped into the room. What was it about those little plastic masks that made people look even worse than they really were?

Jenny was virtually cocooned in those white cotton thermal blankets that hospitals use. She'd been dozing as they came in, but as soon as the nurse finished taking her vital signs, Jenny pulled off the oxygen mask and smiled at Liza.

"They told me I was exhausted when I got in here, then it seems like they've been shaking me awake about every ten minutes, taking my blood pressure and the rest." Jenny did look tired, with prominent rings under her eyes. She was also thinner after her ordeal. And her face was . . . different. Suffering (or maybe enforced maturity?) had refined her features. When Liza first met Jenny Robbins, she'd been introduced to a beautiful girl. Now, however, Jenny had become a striking woman.

She took Liza's hand. "I wanted to thank you for rescuing me."

"Kevin and Michael did that," Liza said, feeling suddenly — oddly — shy. "They're the ones who figured out where you were and went there."

"But they wouldn't have without you to get them started." Jenny's hand tightened. "I didn't know what was going to happen out there. By rights, I should have been terrified all the time, but I wasn't when the big guy — Calvin? — was with me. He was gentle and, I think, sorry for me. And when that man with the gun came —"

She shuddered, and not from hypothermia. "He would have killed me like squashing a bug."

"It's over now," Liza said, soothing her free hand over Jenny's clutching fingers. "Just a bad memory."

Jenny nodded. "At least it's getting there. They told me the bad news about Uncle D. I sort of expected it, that something bad must have happened, when I came back to the house and found those two guys running out."

She looked up at Liza, her red-rimmed eyes suddenly wide. "He told me things had gone very well with you, and I wanted to do something to celebrate. I don't know if you were aware of this, but Uncle D was fanatically careful about his weight. He said I'd have to learn about what a widening experience being on camera could be. Anyway, he never kept ice cream in the house — too much of a temptation, he said. So I went down to town and got a pint of his favorite — mine, too — fudge ripple."

Her eyes filled with tears, and for a moment she was just a girl again. "I'd just parked my car in front of the house when the door flew open and two men came running out. I was afraid of the bald one. He kept yelling because I'd seen their faces and waving this little gun. But the big guy told him to shut up — they'd just have to take me along."

She squeezed her eyes shut, then opened them again. "The rest — well, I guess you know. I heard that you caught the bald guy setting a bomb down in L.A."

"And now it's finished. I just thank God you came out of it all right," Liza told Jenny. "If there's anything you need —"

"Funny you should mention that," Jenny's lips quirked into some semblance of a grin. "There's something I need to talk about with you before they come in and throw you out. I don't have a phone in here, but from what the nurses are saying, the switchboard people are getting pretty tired of fielding phone calls." She looked up at Liza. "Most of them seem to be people offering me film deals."

Liza drew out the bulky envelope from the pocket of her suit jacket. "I thought my partner was crazy when she gave me this. But it looks as though I underestimated her." She spread it out, along with a pen.

They had time for some quick discussion before the nurse returned. When Liza left the room, she had a signed contract.

Only when she was out in the corridor did Liza recall what Michelle had said when this all started, when she'd contacted her partner after dinner at Derrick's. Signing that contract didn't just tie up Jenny Robbins. She was going to be *Liza's* responsibility.

*I* really *underestimated Michelle,* Liza thought with a sigh. *Two months in the country, and I've completely lost my edge. Well, I'll have to get it back, and quick. From the sound of things, handling publicity for Jenny will be a full-time job for the near future. And what about my sudoku gig on the paper?*

She shook her head as she headed for the lobby. So much for simplifying her life.

Then, ahead, she spotted the two figures in green scrubs talking with Ava — Kevin, his sandy hair cut to almost military shortness, Michael with his tousled dark curls. One an avid outdoorsman, the other the perfect indoor sudoku partner — both of them darned attractive, Liza had to admit. Each of them had been out of her life, but as they turned to her, both were obviously showing interest now.

Another complication.

Liza hid a grin, refusing to worry about it. If this adventure had proved anything, it had shown that she could solve puzzles. *Now all I have to do is carry that from paper into real life . . .*

She gave up the struggle and smiled like a kid on the last day of school, completely happy for the first time since this whole adventure had begun.

*It should be fascinating!*

# SUDO-CUES

## Could You Solve Tournament-Level Sudoku? Here's the Help You Need to Get Started
*Written by Oregon's own leading sudoku columnist, Liza K*

It's been a while since we've gone beyond the basic techniques needed to solve sudokus. And what better way to see them in action than to solve some puzzles by Will Singleton? These are puzzles the redoubtable Mr. S. unleashed on the contestants at the Southern California Invitational Sudoku Tournament. Puzzle one was one of five designed for entry-level contestants, with twenty-five winners moving on to the more difficult second puzzle to determine the tournament champion. (Yours truly came in second place, ahem.)

Solving a puzzle on the level of puzzle one will call for basic techniques. A puzzle on the level of puzzle two is considerably

295

harder — pretty much a top-of-the-line newspaper sudoku — and requires more sophisticated techniques before it yields a solution.

But I want you, gentle readers, to be able to do both.

So, here we go, technique by technique, from easiest to most difficult. (For reasons that will become clear as we go on, I refuse to use the word "hardest" when talking about sudoku techniques.)

## Hidden Singles

No, despite the suggestive name, this isn't the answer to the question, "Why can't I find Mr./Ms. Right?" A hidden single is the proper value for a space that "hides" among several candidates if you were to list the possibilities — but it stands out easily when you change your focus. I've always called it "scanning for a triple play," and I think it's better demonstrated than discussed.

We know that, running vertically or horizontally, each group of boxes — the nine-space subgrids in a sudoku puzzle — must house three examples of a given value. (Three 1s, three 3s, and so on.) A given number in a box prohibits any more appearances by that number in that box. It also prohibits the appearance of the number in a

| | | | 9 | | | | | 5 |
|---|---|---|---|---|---|---|---|---|
| 9 | 5 | 1 | 3 | | | | | |
| | | | | | | 3 | 9 | |
| 1 | 3 | | | 2 | | | | 8 |
| 4 | | | | 7 | | | | 2 |
| 2 | | | | 8 | | | 6 | 4 |
| | 2 | 3 | | | | | | |
| | | | | | 1 | 5 | 2 | 6 |
| 6 | ? | | | | 2 | | | |

row or column. With that thought in mind, focus your attention on the space marked with a question mark in this puzzle.

From the "list the candidates" viewpoint,

| | | | 9 | | | | | 5 |
|---|---|---|---|---|---|---|---|---|
| 9 | 5 | 1 | 3 | | | | | |
| | | | | | | 3 | 9 | |
| 1 | 3 | | | 2 | | | | 8 |
| 4 | | | | 7 | | | | 2 |
| 2 | | | | 8 | | | 6 | 4 |
| ⊘ | 2 | 3 | | | | | | |
| ⊘ | | ⊘ | | | 1 | 5 | 2 | 6 |
| 6 | ? | ⊘ | | | 2 | | | |

there are five possible values for this space — 1, 4, 7, 8, and 9. Shift the viewpoint, however, and you can cut away this clutter. Check vertically, and you'll see the two boxes above each have a 1. What about finding a 1 in the bottom left box?

The 1s in the first and third columns of the puzzle "claim" two columns that make up the box, as shown by the shading. That means that four of the available six spaces can't take a 1, as shown by the "prohibited" symbols.

What about the remaining two spaces? The box next door also contains a 1, which blocks that number's appearance on any of the spaces in the row it occupies. See the new shading and additional "prohibited"

| | | | 9 | | | | | 5 |
|---|---|---|---|---|---|---|---|---|
| 9 | 5 | 1 | 3 | | | | | |
| | | | | | | 3 | 9 | |
| 1 | 3 | | | 2 | | | | 8 |
| 4 | | | | 7 | | | | 2 |
| 2 | | | | 8 | | | 6 | 4 |
| ⊘ | 2 | 3 | | | | | | |
| ⊘ | ⊘ | ⊘ | | | 1 | 5 | 2 | 6 |
| 6 | ⊕ | ⊘ | | | 2 | | | |

sign on the next page. That means only one space can take a 1 — the one now marked with crosshairs.

This technique is an excellent starting gambit as you pick up a sudoku. If it works, you stand to fill in several spaces. If it doesn't (for instance in puzzle two), you know you're in for a tougher puzzle.

## Naked Singles

Strangely enough, this is not a form of strip tennis or an offshoot of online dating, but rather another good technique for starting out with a puzzle. Some members of Sudoku Nation call it "counting down." Choosing a particular space on the puzzle, you ask, "Can a 1 go here? Can a 2?" and

| 3 | | 2 | 9 | | | 6 | | 5 |
|---|---|---|---|---|---|---|---|---|
| 9 | 5 | 1 | 3 | | | 2 | | ? |
| | | | 2 | | | 3 | 9 | |
| 1 | 3 | | | 2 | | | | 8 |
| 4 | | | | 7 | | | | 2 |
| 2 | | | | 8 | | | 6 | 4 |
| | 2 | 3 | | | | | | |
| | | | | | 1 | 5 | 2 | 6 |
| 6 | 1 | | | | 2 | | | |

so on. It's best to try this abbreviated form of twenty questions (all right, nine) on a row, column, or box that has the majority of spaces filled. When checking the intersecting rows or columns and the overlapping box for answers to your questions, you'll have fewer possibilities to begin with.

We've progressed a little farther along with this puzzle, as you see. Try the technique on the space marked with the trusty question mark.

When you've run through the possibilities, you're left with only one. Fill it in, and let's keep going.

## Nominating Candidates

| | | | | | | | | |
|---|---|---|---|---|---|---|---|---|
| 1 2 3 4 5 6 8 | 1 4 5 6 | 2 3 4 5 6 8 | 1 4 6 7 | 4 7 8 9 | 1 6 8 9 | 1 2 3 4 7 8 9 | 1 2 5 7 8 | 1 2 3 4 5 7 8 9 |
| 1 2 3 4 8 | 1 4 | **7** | 1 4 | **5** | 1 8 9 | **6** | 1 2 8 | 1 2 3 4 8 9 |
| 1 4 5 6 8 | **9** | 4 5 6 8 | **2** | 4 7 8 | **3** | 1 4 7 8 | 1 5 7 8 | 1 4 5 7 8 |
| 1 4 5 6 7 8 | **2** | 4 5 6 8 | 3 4 5 6 | 3 4 | 5 6 | 1 3 7 8 | **9** | 1 3 7 8 |
| 4 5 6 9 | 4 5 6 | 4 5 6 9 | **8** | **1** | **7** | 2 3 | 2 5 6 | 2 3 5 6 |
| 1 5 6 7 8 9 | **3** | 5 6 8 9 | 5 6 | 2 9 | 2 5 6 9 | 1 2 7 8 | **4** | 1 2 5 6 7 8 |
| 2 5 6 7 | **8** | 2 5 6 | **9** | 2 7 | **4** | 1 2 7 | **3** | 1 2 6 7 |
| 2 3 4 7 9 | 4 7 | **1** | 3 7 | **6** | 2 8 | **5** | 2 7 8 | 2 4 7 8 9 |
| 2 3 4 5 6 7 9 | 4 5 6 7 | 2 3 4 5 6 9 | 1 3 5 7 | 2 3 7 8 | 1 2 5 8 | 1 2 4 7 8 9 | 1 2 6 7 8 | 1 2 4 6 7 8 9 |

300

This column has always been strictly apolitical, no Republicans or Democrats involved. The only candidates you'll see here are suggested values for various spaces. Using this technique calls for a sharp pencil to write in small notations for possible values in each box. The way some newspapers shrink their puzzles to almost postage-stamp size, you're lucky to fill in the actual answers. Many thanks to the *Oregon Daily* for giving us enough space to work in. Anyhow, here is puzzle two in all its debut splendor, with the candidates for each space in a type size that hopefully won't cause early blindness.

Yes, it's tedious, but this is where the real work begins in solving sudoku. Every technique from here on aims at reducing those

| | | | | | | | | |
|---|---|---|---|---|---|---|---|---|
| 1 2 3 / 4 5 6 / 8 | ①4 5 / 6 | 2 3 4 / 5 6 8 | 1 4 6 / 7 | 4 7 8 / 9 | 1 6 8 / 9 | 1 2 3 / 4 7 8 / 9 | 1 2 5 / 7 8 | 1 2 3 / 4 5 7 / 8 9 |
| 1 2 3 / 4 8 | ①4 | **7** | 1 4 | **5** | 1 8 9 | **6** | 1 2 8 | 1 2 3 / 4 8 9 |
| 1 4 5 / 6 8 | **9** | 4 5 6 / 8 | **2** | 4 7 8 | **3** | 1 4 7 / 8 | 1 5 7 / 8 | 1 4 5 / 7 8 |
| ①4 5 / 6 7 8 | **2** | 4 5 6 / 8 | 3 4 5 / 6 | 3 4 | 5 6 | 1 3 7 / 8 | **9** | 1 3 7 / 8 |
| 4 5 6 / 9 | 4 5 6 | 4 5 6 / 9 | **8** | **1** | **7** | 2 3 | 2 5 6 | 2 3 5 / 6 |
| ①5 6 / 7 8 9 | **3** | 5 6 8 / 9 | 5 6 | 2 9 | 2 5 6 / 9 | 1 2 7 / 8 | **4** | 1 2 5 / 6 7 8 |
| 2 5 6 / 7 | **8** | 2 5 6 | **9** | 2 7 | **4** | 1 2 7 | **3** | 1 2 6 / 7 |
| 2 3 4 / 7 9 | 4 7 | ①  | 3 7 | **6** | 2 8 | **5** | 2 7 8 | 2 4 7 / 8 9 |
| 2 3 4 / 5 6 7 / 9 | 4 5 6 / 7 | 2 3 4 / 5 6 9 | 1 3 5 / 7 | 2 3 7 / 8 | 1 2 5 / 8 | 1 2 4 / 7 8 9 | 1 2 6 / 7 8 | 1 2 4 / 6 7 8 / 9 |

clumps of candidates to the one true value that must fill a given space. You'll need sharp eyes as well as a sharp pencil to keep updating the incredible shrinking candidates as they are eliminated either by the appearance of true values or by various techniques along the way.

## Row and Box/Column and Box Interactions

Finally, a technique I can name without having all of you out there snickering at the implied innuendos. Sudoku techniques can't all have sexy names. Another way of looking at this might be "lining up the candidates." When you were searching for hidden singles, you relied on the interaction between blocks and rows or columns. As you try it, you may find yourself swearing because those interactions lead you to boxes where there are two or three possible spaces for a value, instead of the one you were hoping for. However, frustration in that technique offers the chance for subtraction in this one.

Look at the way the value 1 distributes itself among the left-hand set of vertical boxes. In the bottom box, it's one of the givens, eliminating any other appearances there and prohibiting 1s in the rest of column three, which is shaded in gray. In the middle box, 1s appear in column one where they're circled and the column shaded. That means that for the top left box, 1 can only be found in column two, where right now there are two competing spaces.

After eliminating the 1s in the first column of box one, look across on the top tier of boxes. The top two rows of the middle box contain 1s, but not in row three. In fact, the only place where 1s appear in that row now is in the right-hand box. That allows you to eliminate all the 1 candidates in the top two rows of that box as shown in the next diagram.

Look now across the bottom tier of boxes. The left-hand box has a solid value estab-

| | | | | | | | | |
|---|---|---|---|---|---|---|---|---|
| 2 3 4 5 6 8 | 1 4 5 6 | 2 3 4 5 6 8 | 1 4 6 7 | 4 7 8 9 | 1 6 8 9 | 2 3 4 7 8 9 | 2 5 7 8 | 2 3 4 5 7 8 9 |
| 2 3 4 8 | 1 4 | **7** | 1 4 | **5** | 1 8 9 | **6** | 2 8 | 2 3 4 8 9 |
| 4 5 6 8 | **9** | 4 5 6 8 | **2** | 4 7 8 | **3** | 1 4 7 8 | 1 5 7 8 | 1 4 5 7 8 |
| 1 4 5 6 7 8 | **2** | 4 5 6 8 | 3 4 5 6 | 3 4 | 5 6 | 1 3 7 8 | **9** | 1 3 7 8 |
| 4 5 6 9 | 4 5 6 | 4 5 6 9 | **8** | **1** | **7** | 2 3 | 2 5 6 | 2 3 5 6 |
| 1 5 6 7 8 9 | **3** | 5 6 8 9 | 5 6 | 2 9 | 2 5 6 9 | 1 2 7 8 | **4** | 1 2 5 6 7 8 |
| 2 5 6 7 | **8** | 2 5 6 | **9** | 2 7 | **4** | 1 2 7 | **3** | 1 2 6 7 |
| 2 3 4 7 9 | 4 7 | **1** | 3 7 | **6** | 2 8 | **5** | 2 7 8 | 2 4 7 8 9 |
| 2 3 4 5 6 7 9 | 4 5 6 7 | 2 3 4 5 6 9 | 1 3 5 7 | 2 3 7 8 | 1 2 5 8 | ①2 4 7 8 9 | ①2 6 7 8 | ①2 4 6 7 8 9 |

lished in the third space of row eight. The middle box has two possible spaces that could have 1s in row nine. That means, by process of elimination, row seven holds the only possible spaces for 1s in the right-hand box. I can see you're thinking, "Very nice, but is there a point to all of this?"

Here it comes. As this version of the puzzle shows, we can clear away a lot more of the candidate underbrush using this technique. But all the 1s we pruned back created an interesting situation in the shaded space in the following diagram. In column eight, we have only a single candidate left for the value of 1 — right there in row three. That value gets inked in, two more 1 candidates are removed from the spaces flanking it in the row, and we only have sixty more spaces to fill. Yes, it's slow. Get used to it.

## Naked Pairs

This is *not* what happens when naked singles get together on the Internet. Naked pairs occur when two spaces in a row, column, or box hold two (and only two) matching candidates. The logic here is pretty straightforward. If spaces three and five offer a choice between 7 and 9, a 7 in space three means a 9 in space five — and vice versa.

There's a naked pair hanging out shamelessly in row two, at columns two and four. Since these spaces prohibit any other ap-

| | | | | | | | | |
|---|---|---|---|---|---|---|---|---|
| 2 3 4 5 6 8 | 1 4 5 6 | 2 3 4 5 6 8 | 1 4 6 7 | 4 7 8 9 | 1 6 8 9 | 2 3 4 7 8 9 | 2 5 7 8 | 2 3 4 5 7 8 9 |
| 2 3 4 8 | 1 4 | **7** | 1 4 | **5** | 1 8 9 | **6** | 2 8 | 2 3 4 8 9 |
| 4 5 6 8 | **9** | 4 5 6 8 | **2** | 4 7 8 | **3** | 1 4 7 8 | 1 5 7 5 | 1 4 5 7 8 |
| 1 4 5 6 7 8 | **2** | 4 5 6 8 | 3 4 5 6 | 3 4 | 5 6 | 1 3 7 8 | **9** | 1 3 7 8 |
| 4 5 6 9 | 4 5 6 | 4 5 6 9 | **8** | **1** | **7** | 2 3 | 2 5 6 | 2 3 5 6 |
| 1 5 6 7 8 9 | **3** | 5 6 8 9 | 5 6 | 2 9 | 2 5 6 9 | 1 2 7 8 | **4** | 1 2 5 6 7 8 |
| 2 5 6 7 | **8** | 2 5 6 | **9** | 2 7 | **4** | 1 2 7 | **3** | 1 2 6 7 |
| 2 3 4 7 9 | 4 7 | **1** | 3 7 | **6** | 2 8 | **5** | 2 7 8 | 2 4 7 8 9 |
| 2 3 4 5 6 7 9 | 4 5 6 7 | 2 3 4 5 6 9 | 1 3 5 7 | 2 3 7 8 | 1 2 5 8 | 2 4 7 8 9 | 2 6 7 8 | 2 4 6 7 8 9 |

pearances of 1 and 4, you can eliminate these numbers from the candidate lists in three other spaces, as shown.

If you really want to get kinky, consider the naked triple. This involves three spaces holding pairs of numbers which will eliminate three candidates from a row, column, or box. They're a bit harder to spot, even though they're out in plain sight. Resolving the naked pair we just discussed actually helps to create some of this three-way action. We're going to fast-forward slightly on the puzzle, clearing away a few more candidates. (Trust me, it's valid. We'll discuss the technique shortly.)

Look down column six. In the previous puzzle version, we removed a 1 in row two,

| | | | | | | | | |
|---|---|---|---|---|---|---|---|---|
| 2 3 4 5 8 | 1 4 5 5 8 | 2 3 4 5 8 | 1 4 6 7 | 4 7 8 9 | 1 6 8 9 | 2 3 4 7 8 9 | 2 5 7 8 | 2 3 4 5 7 8 9 |
| 2 3 ④ 8 | 1 4 | **7** | 1 4 | **5** | ① 8 9 | **6** | 2 8 | 2 3 ④ 8 9 |
| 4 5 6 8 | **9** | 4 5 6 8 | **2** | 4 7 8 | **3** | 4 7 8 | 1 | 4 5 7 8 |
| 1 5 6 7 8 | **2** | 5 6 8 | 3 4 5 6 | 3 4 | 5 6 | 1 7 8 | **9** | 1 7 8 |
| 4 5 6 9 | 4 5 6 | 4 5 6 9 | **8** | **1** | **7** | 2 3 | 2 5 6 | 2 3 5 6 |
| 1 5 6 7 8 | **3** | 5 6 8 | 5 6 | 2 9 | 2 5 6 9 | 1 7 8 | **4** | 1 5 6 7 8 |
| 2 5 6 | **8** | 2 5 6 | **9** | 2 7 | **4** | 1 2 7 | **3** | 1 2 6 7 |
| 2 3 4 9 | 4 7 | **1** | 3 7 | **6** | 2 8 | **5** | 2 7 8 | 2 4 7 8 9 |
| 2 3 4 6 9 | 4 6 7 | 2 3 4 6 9 | 1 3 5 7 | 2 3 7 8 | 1 2 5 8 | 2 4 7 8 9 | 2 6 7 8 | 2 4 6 7 8 9 |

| | | | | | | | | |
|---|---|---|---|---|---|---|---|---|
| 2 3 4 5 8 | 1 4 5 | 2 3 4 5 8 | 1 4 6 7 | 4 7 8 9 | 1 6 8 9 | 2 3 4 7 8 9 | 2 5 7 8 | 2 3 4 5 7 8 9 |
| 2 3 8 | 1 4 | **7** | 1 4 | **5** | 8 9 | **6** | 2 8 | 2 3 8 9 |
| 4 5 6 8 | **9** | 4 5 6 8 | **2** | 4 7 8 | **3** | 4 7 8 | 1 | 4 5 7 8 |
| 1 7 | **2** | 5 6 8 | 3 4 | 3 4 | 5 6 | 1 7 8 | **9** | 1 7 8 |
| 4 5 6 9 | 4 5 6 | 4 5 6 9 | **8** | **1** | **7** | 2 3 | 2 5 6 | 2 3 5 6 |
| 1 7 | **3** | 5 6 8 | 5 6 | 2 9 | 2 9 | 1 7 8 | **4** | 1 5 6 7 8 |
| 2 5 6 | **8** | 2 5 6 | **9** | 2 7 | **4** | 1 2 7 | **3** | 1 2 6 7 |
| 2 3 4 9 | 4 7 | **1** | 3 7 | **6** | 2 8 | **5** | 2 7 8 | 2 4 7 8 9 |
| 2 3 4 6 9 | 4 6 7 | 2 3 4 6 9 | 1 5 | 2 3 7 8 | 1 5 | 2 4 7 8 9 | 2 6 7 8 | 2 4 6 7 8 9 |

leaving only 8 and 9 as candidates there. Farther down the column in row six there are a 2 and 9, while in row eight we find a 2 and an 8. The choices here create a chain of logic that loops between all three locations. An 8 in row two means a 2 in row eight and a 9 in row six. A 9 in row two means a 2 in row six and an 8 in row eight. You can see how one choice forces the others. The chain also forces two candidates out of the clump in column six, row one — as shown below.

## Hidden Pairs

No, they're not carrying on behind everyone's backs. A hidden pair represents two spaces with the same two candidates — and the same logical consequences as a naked pair. Unfortunately, the pair is hidden among other candidates in the spaces, which makes these guys harder to spot.

In the next diagram, look down column one to row four and row six. Together, these two spaces hold ten possible candidates. However, they also represent the only two places where the numbers 1 and 7 appear in that column. So six cluttering candidates get eliminated. There are three other hidden pairs to be found — here are some hints. Look for a 3-4 pair, a 1-5 pair, and a 2-9 pairing in the rows and columns.

## X-Wings

This has nothing to do with *Star Wars,* although there is a force involved — a forc-

| | | | | | | | | |
|---|---|---|---|---|---|---|---|---|
| 2 3 4 5 8 | 1 4 5 | 2 3 4 5 8 | 1 4 6 7 | 4 7 8 9 | 1 6 8 9 | 2 3 4 7 8 9 | 2 5 7 8 | 2 3 4 5 7 8 9 |
| 2 3 8 | 1 4 | **7** | 1 4 | **5** | 8 9 | **6** | 2 8 | 2 3 8 9 |
| 4 5 6 8 | **9** | 4 5 6 8 | **2** | 4 7 8 | **3** | 4 7 8 | 1 | 4 5 7 8 |
| 1 5 6 7 8 | **2** | 5 6 8 | 3 4 5 6 | 3 4 | 5 6 | 1 7 8 | **9** | 1 7 8 |
| 4 5 6 9 | 4 5 6 | 4 5 6 9 | **8** | **1** | **7** | 2 3 | 2 5 6 | 2 3 5 6 |
| 1 5 6 7 8 | **3** | 5 6 8 | 5 6 | 2 9 | 2 5 6 9 | 1 7 8 | **4** | 1 5 6 7 8 |
| 2 5 6 | **8** | 2 5 6 | **9** | 2 7 | **4** | 1 2 7 | **3** | 1 2 6 7 |
| 2 3 4 9 | 4 7 | **1** | 3 7 | **6** | 2 8 | **5** | 2 7 8 | 2 4 7 8 9 |
| 2 3 4 6 9 | 4 6 7 | 2 3 4 6 9 | 1 3 5 7 | 2 3 7 8 | 1 2 5 8 | 2 4 7 8 9 | 2 6 7 8 | 2 4 6 7 8 9 |

ing chain of logic. The basic position to look for is two lines, each sharing the same candidate at the same spaces. These positions would form the corners of a square or rectangle. A perfect example would be two sets of naked pairs that happen to line up.

A choice in any corner of this quadrilateral forces a chain reaction among the other corners. Consider what happens if 5 were chosen in the upper left-hand corner:

This possibility prohibits the choice of a 5 in the row across and also in the column down. However, it forces the choice of a 5 in the opposite corner.

Perhaps some arrows will make it clearer.

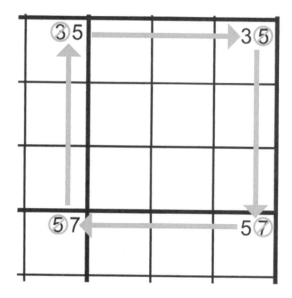

Put another way, this situation creates a logical chain diagonally across the puzzle. If

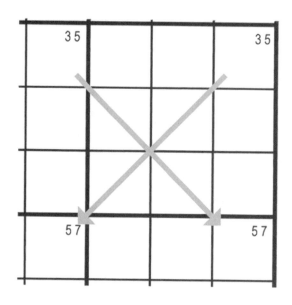

5 is chosen in the upper left, it will also appear in the lower right. The opposite is also true — choosing 5 for the upper right forces the choice for 5 in the lower left. The crossing of those diagonal chains of logic creates an X and gives the X-wing its name. It doesn't just make a pretty pattern, however. Because the given value *must* appear at two corners of the rectangle, it allows you to remove other appearances of the value along the lines making up two of the sides of the rectangle. In the case illustrated to the left you could remove any other 5s from the far columns making the upright sides of the rectangle, as shown.

Unfortunately, real life is often messier than theory. Look at the rectangle formed

| 2 3 / 4 ⑤ / 8 | 1 4 5 | 2 3 4 / 5 | 1 4 6 / 7 | 4 7 8 / 9 | 1 6 | 2 3 / 4 7 8 / 9 | 2 5 / 7 8 | 2 3 / 4 ⑤ 7 / 8 9 |
|---|---|---|---|---|---|---|---|---|
| 2 3 / 8 | 1 4 | **7** | 1 4 | **5** | 8 9 | **6** | 8 | 2 3 / 8 9 |
| 4 5 / 6 8 | **9** | 4 5 6 | **2** | 4 7 8 | **3** | 4 7 / 8 | | 4 5 / 7 8 |
| 1 / 7 | **2** | 5 6 / 8 | 3 4 | 3 4 | 5 6 | 1 7 / 8 | **9** | 1 5 6 7 / 8 |
| 4 ⑤ 6 / 9 | 4 5 6 | 4 ⑤ 6 / 9 | **8** | **1** | **7** | 2 3 | 2 5 6 | 2 3 ⑤ / 6 |
| 1 / 7 | **3** | 5 6 8 | 5 6 | 2 9 | 2 / 9 | 1 7 / 8 | **4** | 1 5 / 6 7 8 |
| 2 5 6 | **8** | 2 5 6 | **9** | 2 7 | **4** | 1 2 7 | **3** | 1 2 6 / 7 |
| 2 3 4 / 9 | 4 7 | **1** | 3 7 | **6** | 2 8 | **5** | 2 7 8 | 2 4 7 / 8 9 |
| 2 3 4 / 6 / 9 | 4 / 7 / 6 | 2 3 4 / 6 9 | 1 / 8 / 5 | 2 3 7 / 8 | 1 / 5 | 2 4 / 7 8 9 | 2 6 / 7 8 | 2 4 / 6 7 8 / 9 |

| | | | | | | | | |
|---|---|---|---|---|---|---|---|---|
| 2 3 8 | 1 4 5 | 2 3 8 | 1 4 6 ⑦ | 4 ⑦ 8 | 1 6 | 2 3 4 5̶ 9 | 2 5 ⑦ 8 | 2 3 4 ⑦ 8 9 |
| 2 3 8 | 1 4 | **7** | 1 4 | **5** | 8 9 | **6** | 2 8 | 2 3 8 9 |
| 5 6 | **9** | 4 5 6 8 | **2** | 4 7 8 | **3** | 4 7 8 | **9** | 4 5 7 8 |
| 1 7 | **2** | 5 6 8 | 3 4 | 3 4 | 5 6 | 1 7 8 | **9** | 1 7 8 |
| 4 9 | 5 6 4 9 | 4 9 | **8** | **1** | **7** | 2 3 | 5 6 2 3 | 2 3 |
| 1 7 | **3** | 5 6 8 | 5 6 | 2 9 | 2 9 | 1 7 8 | **4** | 1 5 6 7 8 |
| 5 6 | **8** | 2 5 6 | **9** | 2 7 | **4** | 1 2 7 | **3** | 1 2 6 7 |
| 2 3 4 9 | 4 ⑦ | **1** | 3 ⑦ | **6** | 2 8 | **5** | 2 8 | 2 4 ⑦ 8 9 |
| 2 3 4 9 | 4 ⑦ | 2 3 4 6 | 1 5 | 2 3 ⑦ | 1 5 | 2 4 ⑦ 8 9 | 2 6 ⑦ 8 | 2 4 ⑦ 8 9 |

from row one, column two, to row one, column eight, to row five, column eight, and back to row five, column two. This is an X-wing for the value 5. Choosing 5 in the upper left prohibits 5s in the upper right and lower left and forces a 5 in the lower right. Or, choosing a 5 in the upper right forces a 5 in the lower left. The point is, this situation allows you to remove six instances of the number 5 from various candidate spaces along rows 1 and 5, as shown. See if you can find a second X-wing in this version of the puzzle. Here's a hint: look for 6s.

## Swordfish

It's not just the title of a confusing movie, it's also the name of a confusing logical loop in sudoku. Just as the notion of naked pairs could be stretched to naked triples, the idea of a four-point logical loop from the X-wing can be stretched to six points in swordfish. And, by working along the involved lines, you should be able to eliminate other instances of a particular value.

We've fast-forwarded a bit in the puzzle to reach a swordfish situation. The swordfish depends on either/or situations for placing the number 7 in columns two, four, and eight.

As the arrows show, choosing a 7 in column two, row one, prohibits a 7 in column eight, row one. This allows us to place the 7 in column eight, row nine, but prohibits a 7 in column two, row nine. In turn, this forces a 7 at column two, row eight, and prohibits a 7 in column four, row eight. This means that however the choice works out, one of two spaces in rows one, eight, and nine will claim the number 7 and prohibit it anywhere else in those rows. This means that you can eliminate the number 7 from among the candidates in seven other spaces in rows one, eight, and nine. Pretty lucky, huh?

This is not an easy concept to comprehend, and I have seen at least one aspiring sudoku solver asking on the Net for explanation/clarification before his head exploded. This is a chain of logic that, instead of an X-wing rectangle, forms an odd-shaped, six-pointed loop. If it doesn't come back around to its starting point, it's not a loop — and you don't have a swordfish.

When you can recognize a swordfish and put it to use, you'll have enough techniques in your arsenal to solve the vast majority of very difficult newspaper puzzles. Certainly, you'll be able to solve the puzzle we're in the middle of right now, although I warn you — there is another Swordfish in your future. There's a little more clearing to be done — consider hidden pairs. Then keep an eye out for 8s, with the loop starting from row one, column one.

Notice what happened there — by using a simpler technique, you help to set the situation for a more difficult one. That's what solving is about — continually cycling through your technique arsenal. After you've cleared away some candidate clutter with a swordfish, you might want to search for hidden pairs or triplets (or even naked ones) to eliminate more pesky candidates. As you eliminate down to one value in some spaces, you may even go back to looking for naked singles as rows, columns, and boxes start filling up. It may take some fairly difficult tricks to get to the endgame, but you usually find yourself using the simplest techniques to finish a puzzle.

There are still higher levels of difficulty in sudoku than the hard newspaper puzzle. In these rarefied realms you might encounter the jellyfish, another closed logic loop — this time circling among eight points. Usually, you can find other, simpler ways to get candidates out of puzzle spaces. You may also have to push the puzzle's logic (and your luck) to find devious solutions.

## Forcing Logic Chains

You might reach a point in a puzzle where you've cleared away enough candidates until you have a bunch of spaces with only two possibilities. Unfortunately, either value could be valid. By focusing on a space and choosing one of those possibilities, you take a "what if" stance and follow where logic leads you — pretty much like knocking over one domino to see how the rest fall. You'll probably end up with an open-ended logic chain that yields a whole lot of possible answers. Then you go back to your starting point, choose the other possibility, and work out the resulting chain of logic from there. It may happen after a few spaces, or you may have to force a fairly long chain. What you're looking for is a point where the two chains intersect — a space where, no matter what choice you make at the start, you find one value that is valid either way.

This gives you the starting point for a new chain of logic — after you've erased the chains of possibilities that led you there. This can be a pretty messy proposition, and it may be better to overlay the puzzle with tracing paper and make your deductions on that. You may want to differentiate your chains of logic by using different colors. Or you can mark candidates by using half circles. Start one chain by drawing a U-shaped half circle under your choices. Set off the next chain by drawing a half circle *above* your number choices. When your chain brings you to a space where you complete a circle, you'll have found what you're looking for.

## Nishio

With this technique, you're not just building a chain but looking for weak links. Again, you're operating in a situation where there are a number of two-choice, either-or spaces. You'll make a choice and proceed on that assumption, looking to see whether the chain of logic you're forcing crashes and burns. Perhaps it will lead you to a space where the only possible answer is already claimed in the row, column, or box. Or perhaps you'll get an answer that eliminates all the candidates in a space.

Either way, you'll know you've gone off on the wrong track. Nishio is not guessing — exactly. Like the forcing chains technique, it's a way to assess the consequences of making a particular choice. Essentially, you're looking for mistakes so that you can eliminate one of a given pair of choices.

The problem is, you can end up developing a fairly long chain before it crashes. There are even some cases where the chain never crashes, and you end up solving the puzzle!

Some people use Nishio as a form of quick check — "Can I get a certain number of valid moves from this choice, or does it quickly self-destruct?" If you decide to try Nishio, you'll probably want to use some sort of overlay. Otherwise, by the time you finish erasing failed chains, your puzzle will look more like modern art than sudoku.

## The Guessing Option (Ariadne's Thread)

If you find yourself in a situation where no technique seems to work and you're forced to guess your next move, you're probably either trying to solve a faulty puzzle — or somewhere along the line you've created a faulty solution. The whole basis of sudoku is supposed to be logic, not luck. Still, if you have no other choice, you might consider an exercise in structured probability. That is, making a guess and keeping track of where it leads you.

Some sudoku theorists give this technique the high-flown name of Ariadne's thread. (In Greek legend, Ariadne gave the hero Jason a ball of thread to help him find his way out of the labyrinth.)

Unlike forcing chains, where you're looking for a particular result, or Nishio, where you're expecting to fail, in this case you're hoping to succeed. Each time you discover a dead end, you backtrack along the line of logic to your previous choice and take the alternate route.

Essentially, it's a case of trial and error, and it's the method most computers use to solve sudokus. In the world of paper puzzles, however, it can use up a lot of pencil lead — and erasers! You'll certainly want to use an overlay to attempt this method. And, unless you're the kind of person who can walk out on a rainy street and immediately hail a taxi, you may not want to depend so heavily on luck.

## Look in the Back

The stricter members of Sudoku Nation may disapprove, but if you're really stuck on a puzzle, why not peek in the back of the book or magazine at the offered solution? Many computer sudoku-solving programs offer a hint option. So why shouldn't paper-and-pencil sudoku addicts take advantage of the same "technique"?

I hope you don't often find yourself in such desperate straits. But remember, sudoku is supposed to be fun, not a source of stress.

Help put the "happy" in "Happy solving!"

# SUDO-CUES

A Look at What *Not* to Do
at a Sudoku Tournament
*Written by Oregon's own leading sudoku
columnist, Liza K*

This weekend I leave the foggy shores of the Oregon coast for sunny La-la Land and a sudoku tournament. The first Southern California Invitational Sudoku Tournament takes place on Saturday at the Irvine Skytrails Hotel near scenic John Wayne Airport.

The SCIST is the brainchild of puzzlemaker extraordinaire Will Singleton, who some years ago decided to graduate from crosswords to sudoku. His puzzles are syndicated all over the country, and if anyone can claim grandmaster status in Sudoku Nation, it's Will. He expects somewhere in the neighborhood of three hundred people to turn up in search of trophies and modest cash prizes. (Yes, modest — which is to be expected. Do the math, people. For a million-dollar prize, the entrance fee for three hundred people would have to be in the neighborhood of $300,000. I'm not willing to ante up to that neighborhood! Are you?)

Sudoku lovers from all over the West Coast will be going for the glory, if not for riches, including yours truly. If I come back with a trophy, you can expect to see a picture here.

Tournament sudoku is still in its infancy here in the USA. However, I've attended more than a few of these gatherings, both here and abroad, and noticed that some of the participants manage to ruin not only their own enjoyment of the competition, but everyone else's, by making some basic bloopers. As a result, I've developed this list.

### Ten Things *Not* to Do at a Sudoku Tournament

1. *Don't forget your brain.* Some tournaments take place over the course of a whole weekend, and some people are so glad to meet other members of Sudoku Nation that they hit happy hour too hard. Hang-

overs and sudoku don't mix. One-day events like the SCIST have another brain-draining drawback — travel. To make my morning flight from the Portland airport, I figure I'll have to be leaving around the same time the party-hearty types here in town will be coming home. I'm really hoping I don't forget to pack my brain.

2. *No artificial enhancements.* In this nip/tuck world where everyone can get a smaller nose or bigger breasts, tournament sudoku requires con-testants to attend as the good Lord made them, at least mentally (the nose and breasts are allowed, if not encouraged). That means you can't come into the contest arena with items like handheld sudoku solvers, or anything that might be used as a sudoku solver, such as laptop com-puters, cell phones, or BlackBerries. Personal digital assistants need not apply. Tournament sudoku is a game for plain, unvarnished brains.

3. *No peeking!* I once attended a fairly crowded sudoku tournament in Tokyo where the guy next to me kept dropping his pencil. I thought

he was checking me out until I realized he alternated between me and the guy on his other side. No, he wasn't an equal opportunity pervert, lusting after both of our bodies. He was interested in our brains — specifically, the brainpower we'd put into solving the puzzles in that round. It didn't help. In the end, Peeping Tomasu got ejected for "causing a disturbance." So don't cheat. And if you're going to cheat, don't use a method that any grammar school teacher can spot.

4. *Don't forget your tools.* Besides banning artificial aids, most tournaments limit the other things you can bring. For instance, the SCIST entry rules specifically state that contestants can only sit down with two pencils and two pens each. A wise competitor not only comes prepared with what's allowed, he/she also checks that those tools work. Pens should be full of ink, pencils should have good points *and* good erasers. Any halfway decent sudoku involves a lot of pencil work, listing possible candidates for

each space. You want to turn in a clean solution to the puzzle. I've seen people lose tournaments because their solutions were ruled illegible.

5. *Don't expect it to be easy.* Okay, you can do every puzzle in *The Complete Nincompoop's Guide to Sudoku.* Does that mean you're ready for tournament competition? Probably not. You won't have enough techniques under your belt to deal with the kind of puzzles serious competitors can solve. The SCIST has five entry rounds. Only five people in each round will graduate to the final challenge. You can expect that people going for the gold (or the gold-tone plastic trophy) won't be finding it easy. My advice? Wait till you can solve the difficult newspaper puzzles — the ones that appear in the Sunday editions — before you go taking your sudoku addiction public. (No, this is not an attempt to clear the field for myself at the SCIST!)

6. *Don't dawdle.* Tournament sudoku is definitely not like the play-at-home version, where you can put

the book, paper, or magazine down to answer the phone or get a snack. Contestants get only forty-five minutes to finish their puzzles. And only the five quickest solvers go on to the next round.

7. *Don't rush.* This may seem contradictory after the last warning. Yes, you want to be in the top five, so you've got to solve these suckers quickly. But you don't want to move so quickly that you miss mistakes in your solution and disqualify yourself. Always budget time to check over your work.

8. *Don't forget the bathroom.* You may be a sudoku whiz, but you won't do well solving a puzzle if you're distracted by — forgive this dreadful pun — the urge to whiz. Tournament officials do not stop the clock in the middle of a competition for bathroom breaks. Do it on your own time, and if nerves send you to the bathroom frequently, take precautions in advance. That third cup of coffee before the competition round might just have unwelcome consequences!

9. *Don't forget your cold or allergy pills.*

When you're racing the clock, you don't want to take time out to blow your nose. The contestants around you won't appreciate it, either, not to mention the distracting effect of disgusting snuffling noises or fear of germs on other contestants — yes, it might give you a competitive advantage, but it also might get you a rep for being a jerk if you show up sick enough to scare people. You want to be at your competitive best, so if you've got symptoms, take a decongestant. Just make sure it's one of the non-drowsy varieties, or you may end up snoozing on your sudoku. And if a decongestant won't control the symptoms, show some kindness to your fellow man and woman and stay home!

10. *Don't forget that you're in public.* Sudoku is pretty much a solitary vice, so people get used to solving puzzles in whatever way they feel most comfortable, even if that way is in their underwear in the privacy of their own homes. In fact, you can get into worse habits than that. Tuneless whistling while you work, tabletop pencil or finger tapping,

leg-kicking victory dances at solving a tough block, or cursing out loud when doing difficult puzzles, for example. These are not behaviors you want to display at sudoku tournaments. And while color commentary might work in baseball or football, it comes off as eccentric when you're doing a puzzle alone — and definitely unwelcome when you're doing a puzzle in public. So spare yourself from getting a sharp pencil in the hand, eye, or heart from your nearest puzzle-solving neighbor. After all, I might be the person on the other end of that deadly implement, and I'd hate to miss out on a tournament because I had to plead temporary insanity to a murder charge. Not that I've ever done such a thing — but I've been sorely tempted. So behave!

I hope to see you at the next sudoku get-together, whether it's local or international. Meantime, happy solving!

# PUZZLE SOLUTIONS

| 7 | 1 | 5 | 2 | 6 | 3 | 8 | 4 | 9 |
|---|---|---|---|---|---|---|---|---|
| 2 | 4 | 9 | 1 | 8 | 7 | 6 | 5 | 3 |
| 6 | 8 | 3 | 5 | 4 | 9 | 2 | 1 | 7 |
| 3 | 5 | 4 | 8 | 2 | 1 | 7 | 9 | 6 |
| 8 | 2 | 7 | 6 | 9 | 4 | 5 | 3 | 1 |
| 1 | 9 | 6 | 7 | 3 | 5 | 4 | 2 | 8 |
| 4 | 6 | 8 | 3 | 1 | 2 | 9 | 7 | 5 |
| 5 | 3 | 2 | 9 | 7 | 8 | 1 | 6 | 4 |
| 9 | 7 | 1 | 4 | 5 | 6 | 3 | 8 | 2 |

*First-Round Tournament Puzzle*
*from page 38*

| 1 | 5 | 4 | 8 | 3 | 7 | 9 | 6 | 2 |
|---|---|---|---|---|---|---|---|---|
| 7 | 6 | 3 | 2 | 1 | 9 | 5 | 8 | 4 |
| 2 | 9 | 8 | 4 | 5 | 6 | 1 | 3 | 7 |
| 4 | 8 | 7 | 9 | 6 | 5 | 2 | 1 | 3 |
| 9 | 2 | 1 | 7 | 4 | 3 | 6 | 5 | 8 |
| 5 | 3 | 6 | 1 | 2 | 8 | 7 | 4 | 9 |
| 3 | 7 | 9 | 5 | 8 | 1 | 4 | 2 | 6 |
| 6 | 1 | 2 | 3 | 9 | 4 | 8 | 7 | 5 |
| 8 | 4 | 5 | 6 | 7 | 2 | 3 | 9 | 1 |

*"Mystery Sudoku" Puzzle*
*from page 136*

| 5 | 1 | 8 | 6 | 9 | 4 | 3 | 2 | 7 |
|---|---|---|---|---|---|---|---|---|
| 9 | 2 | 4 | 7 | 8 | 3 | 1 | 6 | 5 |
| 6 | 7 | 3 | 5 | 2 | 1 | 4 | 9 | 8 |
| 3 | 8 | 1 | 9 | 4 | 2 | 7 | 5 | 6 |
| 7 | 6 | 9 | 1 | 3 | 5 | 2 | 8 | 4 |
| 4 | 5 | 2 | 8 | 6 | 7 | 9 | 3 | 1 |
| 2 | 4 | 5 | 3 | 1 | 6 | 8 | 7 | 9 |
| 1 | 9 | 6 | 2 | 7 | 8 | 5 | 4 | 3 |
| 8 | 3 | 7 | 4 | 5 | 9 | 6 | 1 | 2 |

*"Sudoku 101" Puzzle*
*from page 180*

| 3 | 4 | 2 | 9 | 1 | 7 | 6 | 8 | 5 |
| 9 | 5 | 1 | 3 | 6 | 8 | 2 | 4 | 7 |
| 8 | 6 | 7 | 2 | 5 | 4 | 3 | 9 | 1 |
| 1 | 3 | 6 | 4 | 2 | 9 | 7 | 5 | 8 |
| 4 | 8 | 9 | 6 | 7 | 5 | 1 | 3 | 2 |
| 2 | 7 | 5 | 1 | 8 | 3 | 9 | 6 | 4 |
| 5 | 2 | 3 | 7 | 4 | 6 | 8 | 1 | 9 |
| 7 | 9 | 4 | 8 | 3 | 1 | 5 | 2 | 6 |
| 6 | 1 | 8 | 5 | 9 | 2 | 4 | 7 | 3 |

*"Easy" Article Puzzle*
*from page 298*

| 8 | 1 | 3 | 7 | 4 | 6 | 2 | 5 | 9 |
| 2 | 4 | 7 | 1 | 5 | 9 | 6 | 8 | 3 |
| 6 | 9 | 5 | 2 | 8 | 3 | 4 | 1 | 7 |
| 7 | 2 | 6 | 4 | 3 | 5 | 8 | 9 | 1 |
| 4 | 5 | 9 | 8 | 1 | 7 | 3 | 6 | 2 |
| 1 | 3 | 8 | 6 | 9 | 2 | 7 | 4 | 5 |
| 5 | 8 | 2 | 9 | 7 | 4 | 1 | 3 | 6 |
| 9 | 7 | 1 | 3 | 6 | 8 | 5 | 2 | 4 |
| 3 | 6 | 4 | 5 | 2 | 1 | 9 | 7 | 8 |

*Second-Round Tournament Puzzle*
*from page 301*